THE DARK LADY

(Akala)

Hodder
Children's
Books

HODDER CHILDREN'S BOOKS

First published in Great Britain in 2021 by Hodder and Stoughton

3 5 7 9 10 8 6 4 2

Text copyright © Akala, 2021
Jacket art copyright © Kingsley Nebechi, 2021
Additional images copyright © Shutterstock.com

A CIP catalogue record for this book is available from the British Library.

ISBN: 978 1 444 94369 6

Typeset in Berkeley Oldstyle by Avon DataSet Ltd,
Bidford-on-Avon, Warwickshire

Printed and bound in Great Britain by Clays Ltd, Elcograf S.p.A.

The paper and board used in this book are made from wood
from responsible sources.

Hodder Children's Books
An imprint of Hachette Children's Group
Part of Hodder and Stoughton
Carmelite House
50 Victoria Embankment
London EC4Y 0DZ

An Hachette UK Company
Hachette.co.uk

www.hachettechildrens.co.uk

To my mum

The violence, the stink and [illegible] ... making. We asked as I could see ... [illegible] to get. It was in a quiet place. It say ... [illegible] ... and told him that one [illegible]

The violence, the stink and the slang in the story that
follows are as close as I could get to Elizabethan England.
It was not a pretty place. If any of the words are unfamiliar,
you can find a list with modern equivalents on page 303.

It is said the general is cursed.

L ondon stank.

And even though Henry had lived in London all of his life, he had never really got used to it. The constant whiff that hit his nose like a dull ache all year round, which in these warmer months turned into a sharp burn that seemed to singe the hairs in his nostrils. After all his fifteen summers, Henry was still revolted by the sewage rotting in the sun and the layer of steaming shit wafting up from the waste-filled Thames. Yet Henry also looked on the smells and squalor with fondness. In the mountains of litter from busy markets and slum houses, he saw potential. London – or Romeville, as street kids like Henry called it – offered opportunities, even to poor people, even to thieves.

Henry sat with Mary and Matthew on the roof of St Paul's Cathedral, his feet dangling over the side as he looked out over the city. Henry watched a group of birds pecking at the tiles, wishing he could fly. He looked to the ships on the Thames, and an idea for a sonnet came to him. He'd been obsessed with making up and memorising sonnets and poems for as long as he could remember. The words just seemed to flash into his head. Carefully counting the syllables, Henry mumbled a few lines.

The bird and the ship, the ship and the bird
One that is free because of its nature
The bird and the ship, the ship and the bird
One is man-made, thus destined to failure

He scanned the horizon looking for some more inspiration.

'That's the *Rainbow*,' he said to Mary and Matthew, pointing to a large warlike ship on the water. It had a mean-looking rectangular shape, with a criss-cross of masts and sails, and cannons pointed eagerly in every direction. 'It weighs four hundred and eighty tons and was designed by Matthew Baker to help defend us against the Spaniards.'

Henry gestured towards another, smaller, rounder ship. 'And that one there is called the *Moon*. It's a hundred-ton race-built galleon that belongs to the Rome-mort.'

'We get it, Henry, you like ships,' Matthew said. His round, pale face puffed up around the eyes and his cheeks wobbled as he spoke, which often made Henry want to laugh.

'Ay cousin, no need to be a knave. Don't you two ever want to travel one day?'

'I dunno,' Mary cut in. 'I've heard only ill stories about the seas. Crickets cry.'

Matthew flung his hands into the air. 'Henry and his dreams.'

'So what if I dream? Only people that dream ever make any serious shells,' Henry snapped, but softened his tone to Mary. 'And we all have to die sometime.'

'You know what I mean. People die at sea a lot – and in

ungodly ways,' Mary replied, crossing herself with her hand.

'Ay, I have heard the same, but you can't spend your days fearing death. Otherwise you will never do anything. You could stay in Romeville, get struck by plague and then what?'

'Sooth,' Matthew admitted, nodding.

Henry looked to the swell of tiny people in the tangle of cobbled streets far below and wondered what their dreams might be. He took a chunk of stale bread from his pocket, ripped off a piece each for Mary and Matthew and kept the rest for himself.

'But I am still scared of the sea,' Mary said, laughing, flakes of bread falling out of her mouth as she spoke.

'I'm going to travel on those boats one day,' Henry told them, picturing the images he had collected in his mind from the stories of sailors and the countless books he had read.

'I'm sure you will,' Mary said.

'The great captain Henry and his little mort Mary.' Matthew pushed Mary's arm playfully.

'Dun ure mouse, cousin,' Henry said.

'Yeah, shut up,' Mary added.

'Pish, we all know Henry fancies himself as a globe-trotting outlaw – and you'd love to be his mort,' Matthew teased Mary.

'I'm a more better foister than you'll ever be.'

'Then why don't you put your bit where your mouse is?' Matthew fired back.

Henry spotted a black flag fluttering in the breeze above the Globe theatre.

'A black flag means a tragedy play today,' Henry said.

'That's right, change the subject.'

'I'll bet it's a Shakespeare. Let's go!' Henry said.

'But we don't have any shells,' Mary pointed out.

Henry looked to Mary with a sly smirk and raised eyebrows.

'Well, I'm not into any of that Shakespeare pish, but I'm always up for catching a coney,' Matthew said. He nodded at Henry. 'Show this knave who's really the better foister.'

'To the bridge,' Mary said.

'To the bridge,' Henry and Matthew replied.

The three pulled their dangling legs in from over the edge of St Paul's and turned to walk back across the roof. It was packed with people. A group of finely clad men and women were sat having a picnic. The sight made Henry think on his own clothes: filthy, holey rags that he wore for months on end. His shoes – if you could call them that – were rotten, half-eaten by whatever creatures could get at them in the night. Whereas these people wore velvet or Spanish leather shoes, and outfits in a festival of colours and styles. Most of the women hid their faces in brightly patterned masks to protect themselves from the sun.

But there was one woman who really stuck out to Henry. She was not wearing a mask and she had the kind of arrogant upper-class beauty that drove slum boys wild. Henry had always thought that women like her were so unattainable, like a marble statue, or a palace, that it made them unbearably attractive. She was tall and elegant; every feature from her nose to her fingers looked as if it had been finely crafted. Her black hair had a kept thickness that only wealthy women could hope for. She was wearing a thin cloak made of a new material called silk. Henry had read about this material; apparently it was made by special worms, though nobody believed him when he told them that.

The group was laughing and joking and their picnic was a lavish spread of wine, cheeses, freshly baked bread and many kinds of exotic fruit that Henry had never even seen before. Henry's stomach screamed at him to rob them, but he hadn't missed the armed guards standing nearby. His inner voice dared him to pluck up the courage to talk to the woman, even though he knew how ridiculous an idea that was.

One of the men noticed Henry staring at the lady in the silk cloak and pointed at him. 'Oh look, a Moor!' he shouted. His friends all burst out with laughter, including the lady in the silk cloak. Henry flinched and readied himself to say something back but felt a light touch on his arm from Matthew.

'Ignore those apple-squires,' Matthew said and Henry carried on walking.

They climbed down the stairs of St Paul's and towards the front entrance of the church, each saying a quick prayer as they left and using a hand to make the shape of a cross. They walked down Paul's Chain and turned right, passing lanes that all looked pretty much the same, lined with small taverns and inns, churches and tradesmen. They passed through the French Quarter, where the shop names were written in French.

'What does that say, Henry?' Mary asked, excitedly pointing to the name of one shop.

'Here we go again,' Matthew said with a grunt. 'Yes yes, Henry's got a magic gift, Henry can close his eyes and read languages. In all these years, ain't you bored of it yet?'

'Why you turned Turk today?' Henry shot back.

'I'm just gleeking you cousin, cor, take a joke. Go on, tell her what it says,' Matthew replied with a wave of the hand.

Henry looked up and stretched out his open palm to face the sign, then closed his eyes and breathed deeply. The letters began to appear to him as bright colours and shapes, sounds and musical notes, eventually turning themselves into letters and then words that Henry understood. He opened his eyes and felt the small shock that always came after he used his gift. It was like a giant bee-sting covering his whole body, uncomfortable more than painful, sharp and sudden.

'The Black Hound,' he said, 'it's called The Black Hound.'

'What about that one?' Mary pointed to another shop and Henry repeated the process.

'The Red Lion,' Henry said.

'What abo—'

'Oh come on, how many times we gonna play this game?' Matthew cut in. 'Ain't we got a coney to catch?'

'Fair play.' Henry smiled and punched Matthew in the arm. They carried on walking until they arrived at the bridge.

The bridge was overloaded with shops and five-storey houses that nearly met one another at the top, casting dark shadows across much of the ground, even at midday, and making it a perfect place for thieves. The bridge was also home to Nonsuch House; a massive, almost castle-like building that had been made in Holland and shipped plank by plank to London. Henry had spent many of his childhood hours staring at Nonesuch, wondering how such things could be made, as he often did with many other fine buildings.

'Singing or acting?' Mary asked.

The two boys grinned. 'Singing,' they called, touching palms in the air.

'OK,' said Mary, 'I'll go over there.' She pointed to the square, a large open gap left by houses that had collapsed some years ago and where stalls were now lined up in rows at an angle, leaving an open half-square in the middle for crowds to gather. The three of them huddled together and did their special handshake of thumbs and fingers interlocking followed by a touch of the palms in the air and a brush of the elbows on the end. 'Foisters up!' all three of them said, before splitting up.

Henry scanned the crowd. For him, there was always something in a person's aura that gave them away as a potential victim. Some people had a manner, a kind of sharpness of the eye that said they had their wits about them. But some other people had a certain look that just screamed 'rob me'.

Henry kept walking and scanning. *Bingo.* He spotted a man stood nearby. Henry smiled. The man looked dopey but also too arrogant to know that he was dopey. *Perfect.*

This man will be my theatre ticket, Henry thought as he glanced across at Mary and nodded. Mary nodded back, stood on an empty crate and began singing. Mary's voice washed over the crowd and even tough Londoners used to every scam in the book were mesmerised. Henry laughed at the cheek of Mary's song – an anti-thieving ballad he knew well.

My masters and friends and good people draw near,
And look to your purses, for that I do say . . .

Mary's voice was loud and powerful, with the depth of a woman thirty years her senior, but it also had the delicate touch of youth and the hint of a cry within. Atop the crate, Mary could also keep watch, ready to create another distraction should the boys' potential victims feel themselves being robbed and shout, 'Stop, thief!'

The two words most dreaded by criminals everywhere could lead to a good beating from an angry crowd, and even death.

Indeed, Henry had seen his friend Billy beaten to death by a furious mob after being caught stealing a man's purse. They'd gone to the fair to steal together. He could easily have been caught too. Henry still felt guilt for not being able to save Billy, even though they'd been only eight years old at the time. Memories of Billy's swollen, lifeless face often appeared to Henry when he was about to steal, urging him to be extra vigilant.

Henry's heart raced; his mouth went dry as he walked through the crowd following his target. He fingered his pocket knife affectionately – the blade was freshly sharp. Henry looked to Mary again as she sang.

And though little money in them you do bear,
It cost more to get, than to lose in a day.

Henry turned back to his victim, who was lost, staring at the pretty little street girl with the voice of an angel. He tracked the man, staying close enough not to lose him, but not so near that his intentions would become obvious. It was almost time to strike.

Youth, youth, thou hadst better been starved by the nurse,
Than live to be hanged for cutting a purse.

As Mary finished the verse, the crowd applauded. A few people even threw some meagre coins at her feet. The man put his bags down and took out his purse. He threw Mary a halfpenny before returning his purse to his waist and picking up his master's shopping.

Mary started singing again, adding a little flourish that was just to show off. Henry came up from behind, bumped into his victim and sneaked his hand inside the man's coat. As Henry located the purse string and went to cut it he remembered his training on the bell pocket. His teacher, the legendary outlaw Moll Cutpurse, would hang a coat on a door and put some coins inside a purse in the coat pocket. She would also hang sensitive bells from the pocket and then train the young thieves to remove the coins or cut the purse string without making any of the bells ring. Henry had always been one of the best at it.

Back on the bridge, he cut the leather cord that held the man's money pouch to his large waist with speed and precision, drew the knife back into his pocket as quickly as he had pulled it out and caught the dropping purse with his other hand.

'Watch it, you breechless knave,' the man said. He pushed Henry but only slightly, his bags preventing him from mustering force.

'I am so sorry, sir,' Henry said in a mocking tone, knowing that the man would only hear fear and respect.

'Well, just watch where you are going next time.' The man spoke with all the smug arrogance Henry expected.

'I entreat thee to watch your stamps too, sir,' Henry said, smiling inside at his own cheekiness.

'What?' demanded the man.

'Nothing sir. Sorry, sir,' Henry replied.

The man eyed Henry one last time and then marched off. Henry made his way back to the north side of the bridge to meet Mary and Matthew.

They headed down an alleyway to count their takings. Henry opened the satin pouch with such fury he almost ripped it, emptying the coins into Mary's outstretched hand and counting them out. One pound, twelve shillings and sixpence. *A very decent sum of money*, Henry thought. They could buy a modest lunch and dinner for seventeen days and still have eight shillings to spare for adventures.

Mary reached into her pocket and counted the few coins the crowd had thrown at her – seven shillings in total.

'So how much did you get, chief foister?' Henry asked Matthew.

'Don't bate me,' Matthew replied.

'Come on, don't be a jolt-head,' Mary said.

Matthew begrudgingly took a pouch out of his pocket and counted the coins inside it.

'Six shillings total.' Henry laughed. 'Matthew ranks bottom again.'

'Oi, what are you knaves doing?'

Henry stuffed the coins back into the pouch, shoved it down into his breeches and turned to see two large drunkards approaching.

'Get lost!' Henry said, projecting his voice to try to sound older. Even though Henry was tall and strong for a fifteen-year-old and Matthew even larger, the two boys still looked like boys. Grown men had tried to rob them many times before, often succeeding.

Still the drunks kept coming. 'What you gonna do, you little Turk?'

Henry, Mary and Matthew stepped back but they all knew that the alleyway was a dead end, leading only down to the banks of the Thames. They would have to get past these men if they wanted to escape.

The men were so close now that Henry could smell their

funk of stale brew, bad breath and body odour.

One of the men grabbed Mary's arm. The perverted smile on his face exposed his missing and rotten teeth. The dark stare of his bloodshot eyes spoke of a lifetime spent drinking, gambling and beating women and children the way he had certainly been beaten himself by his parents and masters and lords. Henry had met too many of these kinds of men to count.

'Leave her alone,' Henry shouted.

'Or what?' the other drunkard replied. He bent down to pick Mary up by the waist but she pushed his hands off and stood back with her fists up, ready to fight. The drunkard laughed and lurched down to grab Mary again.

Henry drew his blade from his pocket, stepped around the man with cat-like agility and swung a quick, fierce stab into one of the man's bum cheeks. Like most street boys his age, Henry'd had to slash a couple of people before, but this was the first time he had actually stabbed someone. He felt an intense rush of fear but also a strange fascination as he watched the man scream and howl, blood leaking from his backside and staining his already filthy breeches.

At the same moment, Matthew threw a well-placed punch into the face of the other drunkard, who stumbled backwards, grabbing his bleeding nose.

'That's what,' Henry said, trying to sound ruthless. 'Move your stamps,' he shouted to Mary and Matthew. They sprinted out of the alley, leaving the two wounded drunkards in their wake.

As soon as they got near the crowds approaching the bridge, they slowed down, not wanting to arouse suspicion. Henry looked back towards the alleyway but could not see the men coming after them.

'That was a close one,' Henry said, buzzing from the taste of his own bravery. 'Good job I had my cuttle-bung on me, eh? Proper scotched that villain. I saw you ready to give him your one-two combo,' he added, looking at Mary and ruffling her hair.

'And you, what a blow,' Henry said to Matthew.

'You know my skills already,' Matthew said. 'But I must bid you farewell.' Matthew smiled and flung up his hands, mocking the motions of an actor.

Henry dismissed him with a wave, but Matthew didn't leave. 'What you waiting for?' Henry asked.

'Come on, don't be a jolt-head,' Matthew said.

Henry looked around, feigning confusion.

'Don't play, I want my shells.'

'He wants *his* shells,' Henry said to Mary, pointing at Matthew repeatedly. 'He comes in last as always, but he wants . . . his . . . cut.'

'He only wants to go to the stews,' Mary said, laughing.

'Dun ure mouse, Mary, the joke is getting old now.' Matthew screwed up his face in a mock laugh. 'I might not be as good at picking pockets as you, Henry, but who brings you the best kens to mill from, eh?'

Henry thought through the lucrative house robberies they

had done thanks to tip-offs from Matthew. 'True,' Henry replied. 'We are only winding you up, cousin. Unbend yourself.' Henry opened the pouch, keeping it close to his chest and watching passers-by with a suspicious eye. He passed Matthew some coins.

'Nine shillings? Is that all?' Matthew protested.

'Well, it's more than what you stole for yourself and we need to keep some back for grub,' Henry said. 'And we all know you're going to spend yours quicker than anybody else.'

'Always wagging your lips, ain't ya?' Matthew said, giving Henry a playful punch on the arm. Henry sent a punch back.

'You know I'm right.'

'You lot enjoy the play, yeah,' Matthew said, giving Henry and Mary their special handshake with a 'Foisters up!' shout from them all.

'We will do. You enjoy the stews,' Mary shouted after her brother as he walked off. Matthew stuck his middle finger up at her over his shoulder.

Henry and Mary walked in the opposite direction, but Henry glanced back and saw Matthew throw the piece of bread he had given him on the floor. *The cheek of it*, Henry thought. *He always comes last, we are always hungry and he has the cheek to throw away food.*

As Henry thought about Matthew, he looked at Mary. They were so different, both in personality and the way they looked, that Henry often wondered if they really shared the same father. Matthew was tall and chubby, with pink skin that was almost translucent, his green veins visible just under the surface. When it was too cold or too hot Matthew's whole face turned bright red.

Mary was small and thin with a firm, even complexion. She had long black hair and dark eyes – in contrast to Matthew's blond hair and green eyes.

Henry and Mary arrived at the southern gate of London Bridge. Several severed heads stared back at them from the tops of poles, just lumps of black with no features visible because they had been dipped in tar after beheading.

'Ugh,' Mary grunted and shuddered.

'You know that's what happens to traitors,' Henry said with a shrug.

'How do you know they were really traitors though?' Mary asked.

Henry thought about this. 'Well, I suppose I don't, it's just what people say.'

'People say you're a Turk and a foreigner and that's not true, is it?'

Henry looked back up at the severed heads. He wondered what their names were, whether they had families and if they really were traitors – or if people just said so.

What if the law had been as wrong about these dead men as people are about me? Henry thought. *What if they were killed for no reason?* The thought terrified him.

The south side of the river was another world compared to the inside of the city walls. Sure, the city had its pubs and its drunkards, its duels and its thieves, its public tortures and the hanging post at Tyburn, but the lawlessness down here was so crazy that the south side of the Thames could not contain it, not even inside all five of its prisons. It was here that Henry had got into most of his slashing fights with other boys; it was here that Billy had been beaten to death.

But the south side also had the theatres. Henry and Mary walked along Bankside, through Paris Gardens. Henry admired the manicured hedges and the neatly arranged trees, thinking how sharply they contrasted with the crowds of vagrants, vagabonds and thick-set sailors. Henry took in the range of foreign tongues conversing and haggling, and tried to tune into what he could. Down here on the south side, you had to keep your wits about you.

They passed the bear pit and heard the barking of a pack of vicious dogs, the roars and yelps of whatever bear they were fighting and the cheers and jeers of the gambling audience on the other side of the walls. Mary looked at Henry and then to the bear pit.

'Can't we go in for the bear-baiting first?' Mary asked.

'Nay, the play's about to start,' Henry replied.

'Come on cousin, even Her Majesty the Rome-mort prefers bears to the theatre.'

'Tell you what, let's go and hear this play and I promise to come with you to the bear-baiting later in the week. It's not safe for you to go on your own.'

As if the universe wanted to emphasise his point, at that very moment a topless lady with her head shaved bald was paraded down the street tied to the back of a cart. Henry saw the word 'whore' written in big black letters on her forehead. She had a pleasant face that made her look more like one of his friends' aunties than a prostitute. Her blank expression looked defiant, showing no shame despite the humiliation she was suffering. Henry felt both angry and indifferent. Prostitution was everywhere and everybody knew that, but every so often the authorities picked a random prostitute to punish just to pretend they were enforcing the law. It seemed as if whichever unlucky woman was chosen just accepted her fate as the cost of a life on the streets, and onlookers – like Henry – would never do anything to help these women even though he knew it was unjust.

'Nothing jealous,' Mary said, staring at the condemned woman.

They walked for another minute and arrived at a large white three-storey building with a thatched open-air roof much like the bear-baiting arena.

This was the Globe theatre. Henry's favourite place in the world. A place he saw as magic; a place where writers and actors created whole new worlds from scratch. Henry had been to every public theatre in London but the Globe was the greatest.

Its actors were the best, its costumes the brightest, its crowds the liveliest. And, of course, the Globe had Shakespeare.

As Henry and Mary approached the queue of hundreds, the summer sun still shone in the sky but without its midday intensity. The waning heat made the air less putrid, allowing the scent of trees and flowers from Paris Gardens to battle through the stench.

'The Tragedy of Romeo and Juliet,' Henry read from the display board above the entrance. The people closest to him in the queue shot him a suspicious look. Henry often forgot how strange it was for a masterless man to be able to read.

He watched those who could afford it turn off up the stairs to the boxes and stalls where London's wealthy sat. Henry dreamed of being able to afford to sit in those seats one day. In fact, he had enough money on him now to pay the fee, but if he sat up there in his ragged clothes and half-eaten shoes people would know he must have stolen the money for the ticket.

Henry dropped their pennies into the box and he and Mary entered the theatre with all of the other groundlings, walking into the pit. The atmosphere was enchanting; every seat in the tiers was taken. They tried to get as close to the stage as they could, but the people were squeezed almost shoulder to shoulder. Despite this, young girls managed to snake through the crowd with trays of produce, selling oranges, hazelnuts and oysters. Henry treated Mary to a bag of hazelnuts and an orange.

Ten or fifteen minutes went by and still no actors had come out. Without the distraction of a play, the heat and sweat of the audience was becoming unbearable. Someone threw his apple core at the stage, yelling, 'Come out and save me from these garlic-breathing stinkards,' and the entire crowd laughed.

A minute later, another apple core flew, and then another . . . until a small shower of fruit was raining on the stage. Henry and Mary looked at each other, smiled and both threw their half-eaten oranges to join the downpour.

Trumpets sounded and people roared and stamped and whistled, until an announcer came out on to the stage alone. Everyone fell silent. It was time.

The announcer read the prologue:

> *Two households, both alike in dignity,*
> *(In fair Verona, where we lay our scene),*
> *From ancient grudge break to new mutiny,*
> *Where civil blood makes civil hands unclean.*
> *From forth the fatal loins of these two foes*
> *A pair of star-crossed lovers take their life;*
> *Whose misadventured piteous overthrows*
> *Doth with their death bury their parents' strife.*

The play began, the actors moving on to the stage. Henry turned his ear upwards, stretching his neck, so he could hear the wordplay as clearly as possible and take mental notes. The crowd waxed and waned between noise and silence, disinterested mumbling and complete focus. Henry had been to the theatre scores of times, but he was still struck by the atmosphere and the sumptuous costumes the actors got to wear. These were clothes that only a noble would wear in real life: deep purple fabrics that cost a queen's ransom to dye properly, quality leather boots, jewellery and flashy embroidered silks. As Henry looked to the actors he imagined himself wearing those fancy clothes. And though the swords and shields the actors used in battle scenes were in reality battered second-hand military items, Henry imagined them to be carefully crafted with fine engravings upon the handles and precious jewels set in the middle, awakening his inner warrior.

Henry spent the whole play battling his own emotions. It included many great turns of phrase that Shakespeare was famous for, but Henry did not really like love as a theme. He preferred war, betrayal and the struggles for power that filled Shakespeare's histories.

The play came to a tragic close with the two leading actors – the teenage lovers – dead in the middle of the stage. Henry tried to pretend he didn't care while others in the audience, including many men, cried as they clapped and cheered.

Mary looked at Henry with tears in her eyes. Something about her gaze made Henry uncomfortable.

'What you crying for?' he asked. 'That was some soppy hogwash for Shakespeare.'

In a mocking tone, with grand hand gestures, Henry recited:

My bounty is as boundless as the sea,
My love as deep; the more I give to thee,
The more I have, for both are infinite.

And then added, 'What a load of pish.'

'Dun ure mouse, Henry,' Mary said, wiping back her tears. 'You can't fool me by pretending you don't feel anything.'

Henry felt so naked for a moment that he did not know how to respond.

But, it is said the general is cursed.

*H*enry's mind raced through the day that had just passed. The entire play was compressed into one singular moment. His fight with the drunkards merged with the fights of Juliet's cousin Tybalt and Romeo's friend Mercutio. He saw the cocky, extremely punchable grin of the man who had called him a Moor on the roof of St Paul's. He scanned the ships and the Thames and the shops on the bridge. And throughout all of this, he saw the detail of the faces of every audience member as they processed Shakespeare's words . . .

Then she appeared.

Her black skin was soil, her eyes a thousand lifetimes aged. What has she come for this time? he wondered. Over and over he saw Matthew dropping the bread, his smiling face turning to ash that choked Henry.

'Temper, temper, Henry.' She spoke without a voice.

Henry opened his eyes to find his room as it always had been. The flea-bitten straw mat that served as a bed was the only furniture and even this he shared with Mary and Matthew. When he slept with his head up against one wall, his feet almost reached the other. The smell was soot, urine and tallow.

Henry crept around Matthew and Mary, still asleep next to

25

him, and grabbed his clothes and his rag. He picked out his washbowl and tiptoed down the stairs not wanting to wake Joan and Agnes, still asleep in the other room. Joan was Henry's mother's friend and had adopted him when his mother left; her sister Agnes was Mary and Matthew's mother. The two women could not have been more different – Joan was sweet and wise, Agnes was vicious and cunning – but they were both witches of extraordinary power.

Henry emerged on to the street and looked around at Devil's Gap, the most notorious of London's many slums. The Gap, as most people called it, was well known for producing the city's most feared killers and skilled thieves – outside of the aristocracy of course. Prostitution, poppy dens and knife fights were as common as food was scarce, the buildings were fragile and falling, and the air made the rest of London seem sweet. Nobody came to the Gap unless they had to and very few ever made it out. Yet the Gap was the only place Henry had ever called home.

Life here was short and tough, but today was a beautiful day. It was already mildly warm outside even though the sun was just rising. Henry took in a deep, satisfied breath of air, ignoring the stink for a minute.

The well was just a short walk from the tenements. Henry was surprised to see a mother and her three children already collecting water and washing at this early hour. As Henry lowered his bowl down into the well, he noticed one of the young children staring at him.

The child said something Henry could not quite hear, but by the embarrassed look on the mother's face, it must have been rude. The boy clung to his mother's leg, almost hiding behind it while still staring at Henry. The woman gave Henry a sheepish look and tried to untangle the boy from her, but this only made him tighten his grip. She gave up and carried on washing another one of her children.

Henry stared back at the little boy, taking in his chubby face and his unusually large eyes. He had the look of an old man already and Henry wondered what kind of adult he would turn out to be.

Henry dried himself and got dressed with the boy still staring.

He walked down Eastcheap towards the bakers and felt the city coming alive around him. As the sun rose, Henry studied the people he passed, wondering what they did for a living, where they lived, and whether they were nice or horrible or crazy.

He got to Austin Friars and the Dutch church, another beautiful building that he had spent many hours staring at over the years.

As he looked at the door of the church, a fear grabbed hold of his body so completely that his legs almost gave way beneath him. The words 'go home, foreign scum' were scrawled across the church door in large black letters and the windows had all been smashed. He sat down on the low stone wall that encircled the church grounds to gather himself.

Henry was not a foreigner, but his mother was. He knew

that his brown skin and tightly curled hair made people think that he was too. And the mood towards foreigners had changed in the city over the last few years. He had heard tradesmen and merchants from the Low Countries and refugees from France talk about how they feared for their safety and did not know what to do. Many people felt that foreigners were stealing jobs and the locals had even rioted in protest last summer. The year before, a merchant close to the queen had tried to have all black people deported from England. Luckily for Henry, he was not successful.

He got up and began walking again, but the image of the vandalised church followed him, taunting, like a drunkard's laugh. Suddenly the aroma of freshly baked bread tickled his nostrils and his mood lifted. His mouth filled with water and hunger took over.

Henry reached into his pocket and caressed the money he had stolen, dreaming of the fresh bread and honey he would buy. He breathed more and more deeply with each step towards the bakers. The wafts were so sweet and warm and comforting, it was as if he could taste the bread itself.

Henry joined the long queue and tried to remember the last time he had tasted a freshly baked loaf. It must have been months ago. Like most paupers, Joan could only afford stale cast-offs and she had to make what little they had spread far enough to feed Agnes and the children. Agnes rarely brought any food into their home but always ate more than her fair share. Until yesterday, Henry hadn't stolen for the last few months; Moll Cutpurse had taught him that it was good to have a break from stealing occasionally, lest you grow lazy and get yourself caught.

Henry remembered a poem of Moll's:

> *The greedy thief in hunger for his bread*
> *Becomes so sloppy he loses his head.*
> *Picked a few pockets and don't want to stop?*
> *You'd rather count coin or go for the drop?*

The smell of the bread made Henry wonder why he'd ever gone a day without stealing, if this was his reward. He could not wait to take a fresh loaf back to Joan, because while she would never accept stolen money from Henry, even she could not refuse fresh bread.

Henry thought back to all the times he had brought food into the home, and the plague year when people in London had been dropping everywhere. Everyone had been scared to leave their homes for fear of infection. The whole family had been on the brink of starvation, thin and emaciated, barely strong enough to walk. Henry and Matthew had snuck out while Joan and Agnes slept. They'd crept through the window of a plague-infected house and brought back stale bread, partially rotten vegetables and half a sugar loaf. It'd lasted the five of them two whole weeks. Joan had tried to be angry, but her starvation meant she showed nothing but relief. She'd eaten as greedily as the rest of them and she gave Henry the hug of someone certain that their life had just been saved. Neither Henry nor Matthew ever told her the house had been infected, and luckily neither of them had caught the plague.

Henry remembered the worst winter year when the crops had failed and people starved to death right there on the main square of the Gap. He, Matthew and their gang of thieves had donned masks and robbed a coach of nobles at knifepoint. *Who told them to go prancing around without guards in a famine year?* Henry thought to himself.

Joan knew Henry and Matthew risked their lives so the family could eat and she told them not to steal all the time. But faced with the choice of certain death by starvation or the risk of death by theft, Henry chose to live.

The queue was moving slowly and Henry's belly rumbled loudly but eventually he got to the front. 'Three loaves of white fresh-baked, one granary and a jar of honey please,' Henry said with a big broad smile.

The server ignored him and looked to the next person in the queue. 'What would you like, sir?' he said.

The smile left Henry's face. He looked at the man behind him, then again at the server and repeated his order more firmly. 'Three loaves of white fresh-baked, one granary and a jar of honey please.'

Once more, the server looked over Henry as if he could not see him. The man behind Henry seemed confused, hesitating before stepping forward to place his order.

Henry cut in front of him to try again, but the server continued ignoring him. He hadn't looked at Henry the entire time, even though Henry was staring directly at him. The server had a thin face with a petty, miserly look about it and Henry could feel the hatred in those averted eyes. He wondered if the little, chubby boy at the well would grow into a thin, ugly man like this one.

Henry thought about throwing the large donation plate on the counter in the man's face. 'Call the owner,' Henry commanded, spreading out his arms on the counter to block the next customer.

'My pa is the owner and he is even more loath to your kind than I am.'

The words 'your kind' echoed around Henry's skull. The man had spat out those words as if Henry were a rat infecting the city with another bout of the plague. His rumbling stomach and overwhelming sense of powerlessness made Henry want to beg the server, but his pride was too strong for that.

'I shall not budge. I'll stay here 'til darkmans if I have to.' Henry stared into the man's face, noticing his unusually large Adam's apple. It would make a great target for a punch, and how Henry would like to see this man choke and cough and wheeze from a good strong thump in the throat. Satisfied by the image, Henry was able to soften his eyes, trying to form some kind of human bond with the man. But he would not return Henry's gaze.

It was this that grated on Henry the most. He could deal

with being insulted, but when people acted as if he did not even exist, it vexed him beyond reason.

'What's holding up the queue?' a voice shouted.

'The little foreigner won't move along and nobody is getting anything until he does,' the server shouted back.

'Move your stamps, foreign wretch,' the same voice shouted and a loud murmur of protests and counter arguments started to fill the shop. Some agreed with the man and some were just indifferent and impatient. One man shouted, 'By St George, the Moor just wants to buy a bloody loaf, so let him.' He was greeted with a chorus of boos and jeers.

Finally, the server looked Henry in the face. Now that he had humiliated Henry in front of the whole shop and had the crowd on his side, he was brave enough to hold Henry's stare.

Henry felt breath near his ear and was about to jerk away when a voice spoke. 'Give me the lour and I'll get the bread for you, lad,' the man behind Henry in the queue offered. Henry could tell that the man would not steal his money, and for a moment he thought about taking him up on his offer. But to allow the man to help him would be to admit defeat.

The crowd grew rowdier. The server stood with his arms folded and nodded at Henry, making it clear who the problem was, as if the whole shop had not already noticed him. A group of men outside started chanting anti-foreigner folk songs. Henry could sense the danger brewing in the air.

'Look, lad, if you're not going to let me help you, I would move your stamps,' the man behind Henry whispered. 'You never know what these rascals might do.'

Henry looked through the windows out on to the street at the men's ominous chanting, then back at the server. And for a moment Henry wished that he looked like everyone else. He wished that his skin did not betray the foreign origins of his mother and that he could just be like everyone else. He hated himself twice: once for being different and once more for wishing he wasn't different.

Henry stormed out of the shop, pushing past people on his way, breathing heavily and fighting back tears. The men outside the shop jeered as he walked past them and started throwing small stones. One nearly hit him in the head and one whizzed past his feet, while another glanced off his shoulder. But Henry's pride was too strong to give them the satisfaction of seeing him run away or duck.

He marched down the street, mumbling to himself, wishing desperately that he had punched the server. He felt like a coward for not doing so, even though he knew the men throwing stones would have jumped him had he given them an excuse.

Henry spent the rest of the morning pacing the streets in a hungry frenzy, fantasising about waiting for the baker's son after work so he could stamp on his Adam's apple. He looked around for people to rob or food stalls to steal from, but Henry had vowed to himself not to steal when he was in this kind of a mood. It was the best way to get caught.

He remembered another version of Moll's poem:

The angry thief in hunger for his bread
Becomes so sloppy he loses his head.
A hunger too great? The best cure is bed
All men can sleep but can't eat once they're dead

And he accepted that today would be a hungry day.

War tore a kingdom to pieces.

The kingdom founded by Ewuare the great, eldest son of Ohen.

A woman is cut down by a soldier's blade, a child cries over her

dead mother's body, a husband loses a wife.

Henry loved all sports, but football was his favourite because unlike tennis or bowls or archery, poor people did not get fined for playing football without a licence. All you needed to play football was an inflated pig's bladder and some friends.

Aristocrats did not play football, and this made Henry love the game even more. It was too violent, too common and too cheap for them. There were basically no rules and no designated pitches; Henry had played games of football through narrow lanes, on concrete squares and in open fields – like this one they were playing on today, behind the church.

Henry and Mary's team was winning, and he got more and more cocky with each point. He held the ball tightly in both arms and charged through the other team at will. He saw Matthew approach, ready to defend against him where the others had been unsuccessful. Henry saw everything in minute detail as Matthew charged at him.

Henry dropped the ball to his right foot with perfect timing and kicked it over Matthew's head. As the ball rose into the air, Henry spun round and dodged Matthew's onrushing body, turning a complete circle and running on to catch the ball. Behind him, Matthew fell flat on his face.

Henry ran on to put the ball down in the other team's area,

scoring again. Even Matthew's teammates let out giggles at the breathtaking skill of the move as Matthew got up, his face peppered with dust.

'This is just too easy,' Henry said, doing a little dance to celebrate.

'Dun ure mouse and play,' Matthew snarled back.

'Ooh, touchy touchy,' Henry taunted, ruffling Matthew's hair as he walked past him.

Matthew grabbed Henry's hand, threw it off his head and glared at his teammates. Their laughs turned to grunts as they tried in vain to suppress them.

'Come on, let's get one back,' Matthew commanded in his most leader-like voice.

Henry watched Matthew charge forward like an embarrassed bull. By sheer force he managed to work his way past a couple of Henry's teammates, but more joined the fray. Henry smiled as arms pulled at Matthew's shirt and grabbed at his legs – he was going to lose the ball any second.

Matthew grunted in rage and charged again, but he was going nowhere. He yanked his right leg forward and stamped, trying to get free of the arm clutching it.

A loud scream erupted, Mary doubled over in pain, rolling over on the ground. Henry ran towards her, but Matthew kept charging on with the ball.

'Oi, wait – Mary is hurt,' Henry said as he tried to make sure she was all right. She was gripping her wrist and crying.

Matthew carried on playing as Henry knelt down and

steadied Mary's wrist, trying to ease her pain. 'Stop playing, you jolt-heads. Mary is hurt!' he shouted at the others. Henry's team stopped in their tracks, leaving Matthew free to score.

'Goal!' Matthew cheered as he put the ball down.

Mary's breath was steadying now, but she was still crying.

'My wrist,' she whimpered.

'Goal!' Matthew gloated again.

'Don't be such a boil brain. Your sister is hurt,' Henry snapped.

'This is a big boys' game. Oft-times people get hurt,' Matthew said coldly. 'She'll soon be jolly again. It's just a little bruise.'

Mary let go of her wrist. A large purple and black bruise had already started to form.

Henry felt a stab of anger in his chest. 'No goal,' he said firmly, still looking at Mary's bruise. 'No goal,' he repeated.

'It's a goal,' said Matthew.

Henry stood up and turned to Matthew. 'No. It's. Not,' he said, injecting every word with the air of a threat.

'Yes. It. Is,' Matthew countered, holding Henry's stare.

Henry walked towards Matthew. 'No, it's not,' he said again.

'My wrist is fine by the way, you just worry about that goal,' Mary said, but she may as well have been talking to the wind.

The two boys were face to face.

'Your sister was on the ground crying 'cos you stamped on her foot and all our team had stopped playing,' Henry pointed out. 'Only a lily-livered punk would want to claim a goal like that.'

'Call me what you want. I scored and that's all that counts.'

'It's not a goal, you dogheart.'

'Yeah, a dogheart that just scored!'

"Cos you can only score by hurting little girls, you fat maggot pie.'

Just looking at Matthew was winding Henry up. Henry knew he was better than Matthew at virtually everything – he was smarter and stronger and a more skilful thief. Yet Matthew had a mother that loved him and nobody ever called him a foreigner, even though Agnes was from Germany. He never really had to think about the things Henry went through. And though they were like brothers, Henry hated Matthew for this. Beating him at football was one small pathetic way to get even, but Matthew was too stubborn to give him that.

'What did you call me?' Matthew demanded.

'Fat maggot pie,' Henry repeated. 'A fat maggot pie who's so lily-livered he needs to stamp on little girls to score.'

'Oi, I am not a little girl,' Mary said, 'and I do have a name!'

But Henry was not listening. He knew that Matthew's weight had always been a sore point for him and he watched with glee as Matthew grew angrier and angrier.

'At least my mum's not a black devil that left me when I was born,' Matthew snarled.

Many of the other children laughed and oohed at this. Henry's insides tightened as the words took away his confidence, turning it into a wound instead.

Henry looked at Matthew and saw the chubby boy at the well hiding behind his mother's leg. He saw the baker's son with his large Adam's apple and his ugly, gaunt face. He saw the 'go home, foreign scum' painted on the door of his favourite church. He saw the smug aristocrats that had laughed at him on the roof of St Paul's.

The next moment, Henry's rage overcame him.

He charged at Matthew with all the force he could muster; with all the pent-up aggression of all the times Henry had looked the other way. He saw the fear in Matthew's eyes as he ran at him and this empowered him to charge even faster. Henry threw his entire body into Matthew's stomach, taking him down in one swift move.

He felt Matthew's back hit the dry summer ground and watched the air leave his lungs. But it wasn't enough. Henry climbed on top of him, swinging wildly, hitting at flailing arms as Matthew tried his best to defend himself. Every third or fourth punch would land, bumping Matthew's head up and down on the ground like a ball.

'Stop fighting!' Mary screamed.

Henry's knuckles cracked cleanly on Matthew's nose and it started to bleed. He noticed a small cut leaking over Matthew's right eye where another good shot had landed. Henry smiled to himself. It was as if he were punching back at everybody. His fists were bruised, snot dripped from his nose, yet he kept on swinging, pivoting between smiles of grim satisfaction and cries of wild rage.

'Don't talk about my mum, you yeasty, shard-born foot licker,' Henry shouted through his panting breath.

'Please, stop it!' Mary screamed again.

Taking their cue from Mary, three of the bigger boys grabbed at Henry's arms and started to pull him off Matthew, but this only gave Henry a second wind. He yanked his right arm free and landed a colossal blow on Matthew's left cheek.

Henry felt the boys pulling at his arms again, this time managing to lift him off fully, but as they dragged him back, Henry kicked out at Matthew's lying body with his heel.

Henry watched with great satisfaction as Matthew pulled himself up slowly. He was moving like a wounded animal, his nose and right eye bleeding and his cheek puffed-up from all the bruising. Matthew spat out a mouthful of blood and a piece of cracked tooth.

'Wait 'til I tell my mum about this,' Matthew said.

'Ay, you always were a little mummy's boy who couldn't fight his own battles,' Henry replied.

'At least I've got a mum.' Matthew picked up his ball and limped off into the distance.

Mary got up and hobbled over. 'Don't worry, Henry, I will talk to him,' she said. 'He won't tell Mum. He knows he should not have said that to you.'

'Nay bother. Let him do what he feels. I ain't scared of Agnes,' Henry lied. But he could tell by the looks on everyone else's faces that he'd fooled nobody.

It is said the general is cursed.

Ogun, God of iron and war, is eating well.

H enry felt a mix of pride and disgust as he saw flashbacks of himself punching Matthew. On the one hand he was happy that his fighting abilities were still so sharp, but however much Matthew might annoy him, however cruel his words, they were still like brothers.

Temper, temper, Henry, he told himself.

Henry approached Graham's workshop. As usual, the pungent smell of burning metal seeped out through the door. Henry had always found that strange smell pleasant, perhaps because it reminded him of Graham.

Henry knocked on the door, first gently then louder and louder. After a few tries, Graham answered.

'Come in, lad,' Graham said, removing the thick, filthy cloth that served as his mask.

The brick furnace at the back of the workshop was in full flow, making the room hot and smoky. Graham gestured to a pair of wooden stools and Henry sat down, trying not to choke on the fumes as they tickled the back of his throat and stung his eyes.

Graham poured out two cups of beer and passed one to Henry.

'So, what's troubling your skull, lad?' Graham asked. He

patted Henry on the back of the neck as he walked past, sending a little feeling of comfort rolling through Henry's body.

'Nowt,' Henry said, changing the pitch of his voice to try to sound happy.

'You've never been any good at hiding how you feel, Henry – not from me anyway.'

'I'm fine, honestly,' Henry lied.

'Well, in that case you can help me work, as I'm late on this batch,' Graham said.

Henry went to speak, then stopped himself and just replied, 'All right.'

Graham sat on the stool opposite Henry. Henry fidgeted, tapping his right leg up and down as he sat; he could not stop it.

'Been nice and warm lately, ain't it,' Graham said, more as a statement than a question.

'Ay.' Henry smiled and laughed.

'Makes Romeville stink even worse when it's hot though.'

'Ay,' Henry said again, with the same forced laugh. He took a sip of his beer. 'How's work?' Henry asked.

'Good, good.' Graham got up and rummaged through some drawers. He took out an apron and a mask just like the ones he was wearing and handed them to Henry. 'Put these on when you finish your beer.'

Henry took another quick sip, got up and tied his apron on. He pulled the string of the mask behind his head, resting the face part over his forehead so he could finish his drink.

'Overworked, but it's good to be so busy. It's when the orders stop coming in that you'll hear me start prating like an old mort.'

Henry got the hint, took another sip of his beer and pulled the mask over his nose and mouth.

'I'm ready. How can I help?' he asked.

Graham led the way to the far side of the workshop and the furnace. The room was as big as a small church, and even though they were still a few metres away from the furnace, it was much, much hotter over here.

'See that pot there?' Graham pointed to a large metal tin containing hundreds of sewing needles. 'Take them out and sharpen them on that stone, just like I showed you before.'

Henry got straight to work, taking a needle from the tin, grinding the end back and forth on the sharpening stone for a few minutes, then placing the sharpened needle into the tin on the other side of the table. Graham was hammering out fresh needles from hot metal wire at another workbench a couple of metres away. It was tough work even for two men, Henry thought, and he had no idea how Graham did it all by himself.

'How's Mary and Matthew?' Graham shouted through his mask.

'Well . . .'

'Go on, lad, what is it?' Graham's voice had a deep gravel-like quality to it, as if his throat had been scraped by some rough object. Henry found the tone, like the odd smell of burning metal, comforting. When Henry hesitated, Graham put his hammer down and looked Henry in the face.

'I beat Matthew.' Henry spat out the words and hung his head. 'More worser,' he added, turning his hands over to show Graham the knuckle damage.

Henry looked up and the expression on Graham's face confused him. Then he realised he had seen it before on the faces of older men. It was a muted look of admiration. Henry knew that older men were obliged to tell you that fighting was bad, to lecture you on how to behave, to pretend to be disappointed and all that. But the truth was, they always admired a tough kid. Henry could tell that the blood and bruising on his knuckles encouraged respect from Graham and made him think of his own fights as a younger man.

'Why, lad?' Graham asked.

'He . . .' Henry trailed off again. He knew Graham of all people would understand, yet he still felt a sense of shame at the insult, as if he were actually guilty of being a black devil.

'He named my mum a black devil, even after everything . . .' Even though Henry did not finish the sentence, he knew Graham had understood what he had meant. Matthew had seen how Henry had been treated his whole life and he still insulted him despite it. Graham walked towards the furnace and Henry instinctively followed.

'Pass that bucket there,' Graham said, pointing to a bucket full of coke-fuel. Graham climbed a ladder that leaned against the furnace and Henry passed him up the bucket. 'Why did he call you such a thing?'

Henry explained everything that had happened leading up to the fight – the boy, the vandalised church and the baker. Graham took it all in.

'You know, lad, if we take to blows every time we have a tough day or someone insults us, we'll be fighting until the crickets cry,' Graham said as he poured the bucket of coke-fuel into the furnace.

'I know.'

As the fire growled, Henry turned away from its heat. *How can Graham just stand there as if he doesn't feel a thing, right over the hole in the furnace?*

'I understand that it hurts more coming from people we love . . .' Graham looked into the flames, yellow flickers of light dancing on his black forehead.

Henry flinched at the word 'love'. Did he love Matthew? He guessed he did, deep down.

Graham pointed to another bucket filled with limestone and Henry passed it up. Graham poured it into the hole and returned the empty bucket to Henry.

'I've had many a fight with friends in my days. Don't worry too much. Find Matthew and apologise, but be sure to let him know he was out of charge too.' Graham paused. 'Pass me that poker there?' he asked, then added, 'You never insult a man's mother, everybody knows that.'

Henry walked past the ladder, picked up a long metal poker from the corner of the room and passed it up to Graham. 'Sooth,' Henry said, 'but Agnes is going to go bedlam.'

When he and Matthew had fought last summer, Agnes had touched Henry with a spell as a punishment and his skin had boiled up and itched for weeks on end. It hurt far more than any of her many beatings. Another time she had made him stink worse than a cesspit. No matter how many times per day he washed, the smell would not go, until Joan realised what was going on and did a counter spell to cure him.

Henry already stood out enough as it was, without stinking like a raging drunk who'd bathed in shit. It had caused him more embarrassment than he cared to remember.

'She hates me anyway,' Henry said, 'so this will be a great excuse for her to perform more of her second-rate charms on me.'

'That part I can't help you with,' Graham said, poking the furnace with the metal rod. The fire smoked even more, most going out of the chimney, but still a large amount of smoke floated out of the furnace hole, past Graham's face and up to stain the high ceilings of the workshop. 'I am not a charming man and I learned a long time ago not to interfere with other people's families.'

'She is not my family,' Henry countered. The mere suggestion made his nostrils flare.

'Forsooth, son, but they are the closest thing you have. I'm sure somewhere beneath all the chiding and beatings Agnes does love you.'

'That just shows how much you don't know Agnes. She is the Devil.'

Graham climbed down from the ladder and put his hand on Henry's shoulder. 'The Devil is the Devil,' Graham said seriously and made the shape of the cross on his head, chest and shoulders.

'Sooth, but you know what I mean. The woman is evil.'

'What *is* evil?' Graham asked.

Oh no, he is going to go into one of his wise-man speeches, Henry thought.

'Henry, my boy, the world is a tough place, full of rascals and rogues that don't owe you a thing – even when they are raised under the same roof.'

Graham moved to one side of the furnace, in front of a large pipe that pumped air in. Henry knew to do the same on the other side. They each squeezed the bellows attached to the pipes a few times and the fire spat and flickered and boomed.

Graham continued, 'Since the riots against the Low Country folk last summer, the mood in the city has been extra hostile. But I'll tell you, my boy, I'd still much rather be here than back in Spain.' Graham raised his voice over the crackle of the fire. 'In Spain, most of my fellow Ethiopes are little more than slaves, except for Juan Latino of course.'

'Who's Juan Latino?' Henry shouted back, still squeezing the pumps slowly, even though Graham had paused to admire the fire.

'What? Have I never told you about Juan Latino?' Graham asked, not taking his eyes off the furnace.

51

'No, never.'

Graham walked towards Henry. 'I don't believe it. Juan Latino is famous back in Spain. A son of slaves who rose to become a professor of Latin at the University of Granada – and he is even blacker than me.' Graham chuckled. 'He is a legend among black people in Spain.'

Henry stopped pumping, trying to picture a black man teaching Latin at the University of Granada.

'Nothing jealous?' he asked.

'Nothing jealous.'

'Why have you never spoke of him before?' Henry demanded.

'I dunno, lad, I thought I had. The whole of southern Spain used to be ruled by Moors, Berbers and Arabs – some of them blacker than me and Latino put together.' Graham laughed. 'Al Andalus they used to call it, back when my grandad was alive. They built loads of universities and palaces. The best one, called the Alhambra, is still there. But they did not believe in Christ, so it's bitter-sweet, lad. Though Catholics are in charge in Spain now and they're even worse than the non-believers.' Graham crossed himself.

Henry went silent thinking of Juan Latino and trying to imagine Spain being ruled by Moors and Arabs. He was almost angry that he hadn't heard about this before – as if Graham had lied simply by not telling him.

Graham gestured towards the work benches and they moved back over and began again, Henry sharpening the needles and Graham beating out new ones.

'As for the English, lad' – Graham whacked the hammer down between phrases – 'they despise everybody for some reason or other' – he hit the hammer on the metal wire a few times again – 'the poor for being poor, the Huguenots and Low Country folk for being foreign' – *hammer, hammer* – 'Spaniards and Italians for being Catholic,' Graham paused, 'though I must admit I agree with them there. And they misprise us for being black.'

Graham looked at Henry again. 'Well, I'm not quite sure what to call you – brown maybe?' Graham smiled. Henry tried not to show that he was half-insulted even though he knew Graham meant no harm.

Graham was panting between words. 'But it could be more worser. In France they have been massacring Huguenots for years. My ears have it that in Germany they roast poor people and witches alive by the hundreds. And in Spain most people of our colour are slaves and they expelled Jews back in 1492 – along with the Moors. Best not to take it too personally. People might misprise me because I am black yet they still need my needles, don't they? They still come here every Saturday and buy the fruit of my sweat. I am able to feed myself quite well and buy logs for the fire and live a decent life. Get a skill, Henry, a skill other people will pay you for, and your colour matters not.'

Henry looked at Graham with a respectful doubt in his eye. 'Well, it won't matter as much,' Graham corrected himself. *His speech was actually not so bad after all*, Henry thought.

Graham took his mask off and looked Henry right in the eyes. 'And quit the coney-catching crap.'

Or maybe not.

'Yes, lad, don't think I don't hear the ear-kissing about you lot. You will get caught like all thieves eventually do and you will dance on the rope. Besides, you are way too smart for that.'

Henry looked into Graham's face and for the first time he really noticed his age. Graham's effervescence had always made him appear young to Henry but now – as he observed Graham's grey hair, his pain-filled eyes and his rough skin – he knew that he must be in his early fifties at least, making him one of the oldest people that Henry had ever met. Henry suddenly feared that Graham would not be around that much longer, but watching him work with the energy of a man twenty years his junior made such thoughts seem absurd.

Graham led them back over to the stools by the window and poured Henry another beer. 'I have an idea, lad,' Graham said and Henry sensed a triumphant tone in his voice. 'I have been thinking about this for some time actually. I am an old mucker, as you may have noticed. And I am the only one in this city who makes needles of this quality.' Graham plucked one from the table and held it up to Henry as if it were a gold coin. 'If you teach this fusty mucker to read, I'll teach you to make these needles, and when it's my time for the crickets to cry on me you can take over the workshop.'

Henry saw the look of hope on Graham's face. He took in the workshop – the rusty tools, the stained walls and black ceiling, the small mattress of hay little better than the one Henry slept on – and tried to imagine himself in his fifties, living like that. He didn't want to disappoint the old man, but he knew deep down that he would prefer the risks of an outlaw's life to this.

'I'll teach you to read, I'd love to. But I can't take over this place, though I am flattered that you even ask.'

'Why? You think you're too valorous for needle making because you can read? You'd prefer to keep coney catching because that's so honourable a thing? And let me guess, you dream of being rich one day?' Graham threw the needle in his hand across the room.

'I don't think I am better 'cos I can read,' Henry lied. He knew that being able to read was a sign of wealth and power. That's why years ago a man named William Tyndale had been burned alive for translating the bible into English so that paupers could read it. That was why Ben Jonson – one of Henry's favourite playwrights – had been able to avoid punishment for murder by showing the court that he could read. 'But I do have dreams. I want to write and travel and see some more of this orb one day.'

'Dreams?' Graham said the word with disgust. 'Dreams are a fool's errand. They exist only in your head and distract you from the real world, lad. But you are too young to have realised that yet. Look around you. Most masterless men are either on the brink of starvation or they are outlaws. And we know what eventually happens to all outlaws – they dance on the rope. I have my own life, I buy my own bread and I don't answer to nobody.'

Henry didn't want to tell Graham that he saw more honour and glory in an outlaw's death than in taking orders for an entire lifetime and staying desperately poor. As a child Henry had watched many a robber hanged at Tyburn, admiring the way they strutted up to their deaths, sometimes telling jokes and singing, sometimes even throwing flowers into the huge crowds. It was one of the things that had attracted him to stealing. They looked life in the face and they faced death like soldiers. If that was what it meant to be an outlaw, Henry was all right with it – and if it weren't for stealing, Henry would already be dead. It wasn't as if Graham was totally legal himself. Smelting iron right here in the middle of London was a huge fire hazard and totally illegal, and Henry was sure that, like many foreign workers, Graham did not have a licence to sell the iron or the needles. But he could not say any of this to Graham. 'That's all true . . .' Henry began.

'But?' Graham asked.

'But I still have dreams. I don't want to be stuck here making needles.'

The wrinkles around Graham's eyes bunched up tightly and Henry was stung by the pain and contempt on the old man's face. 'By Solomon, you are a fool, son. A high-sighted fool, but a fool nonetheless.'

Henry knew that some part of Graham must admire his conviction, but that did not make it any easier to bear his disappointment.

'Look, think about it, lad,' Graham said, 'but in the meantime I have to get back to work. Some of us need to earn our living you know, stuck here making needles.'

Henry realised he had hurt the old man's feelings by dismissing his trade like that. Suddenly Agnes came back into his mind and fear rushed back over his body.

'I can stay and help,' Henry offered half-heartedly.

'I'll be fine, lad,' Graham said quietly and Henry knew not to push it. He took the last sip of his beer and got up to leave.

'Pass by again soon, don't be a stranger.'

'I will, I promise.'

'Good. See you soon, lad.'

Graham gave Henry a firm hug. Henry turned and left the shop to make his way back home.

He wished he could have stayed in that hug all day.

The general and his daughter flee into the night.

They pray to Shango for lightning and thunder to cover them.

On horseback they cross river and forest and plain.

But it is said the general is cursed.

A large black barbary horse was tied to a tree outside of Henry's home. The horse had a beautiful saddle and the kind of shiny black coat that could only be maintained by an owner who could afford to keep their horse clean and well-fed. For a moment Henry thought about stealing it, but a horse this expensive and rare would be hard to get rid of.

He stroked the horse's coat for a few minutes before finally going in to face the music. He wondered what curse Agnes would place on him this time. Henry didn't go into the small tenement where he, Mary, Matthew, Joan and Agnes all lived, but instead went downstairs beneath their home, where Joan had her apothecary. Henry unlocked the apothecary door and walked down the stairs cautiously, worried that Agnes would be waiting, ready to pounce on him. He turned into the main room and saw Joan sat at the large wooden counter serving a customer, so he stepped back and hid behind the wall. He didn't want to disturb Joan while she was in the middle of an appointment. He peered around the corner and spied on the session instead.

The customer was wearing a red velvet hat and expensive cloak – and Henry guessed that the barbary horse outside must belong to him. The man looked out of place in the apothecary.

The mud walls were covered with a deep green algae, making the room appear like an underwater forest. A large tree grew in the middle of the room, its trunk like a pillar and its branches spread across the celling like veins, bearing leaves even without sunlight. Strange plants sprouted from the walls and behind the desk hung shelves filled with jars of ointments and potions. Despite the candles and brightly coloured crystals everywhere, still the place was dim and dark, but this only enhanced its magical quality.

For longer than Henry had been alive, Joan had been prescribing potions and simples, herbs and healing ointments, astrological affirmations and spells. Her clients were usually paupers, peasants and tradesmen. They would come in with a range of ailments or with bad luck in love or finance or life. The poorer people did not look so out of place in this otherworldly underground forest, dressed in their simple ragged clothes that were not so far removed from nature. But every so often, Joan would have a client like this man – too well-off to share the suspicions of the peasants and too finely clad to be here.

Henry tuned into the conversation Joan was having with her client.

'Take this stone and on the next full moon, bury it in the soil for three days,' Joan spoke in mystical tones. 'When you dig it up, wash the crystal in this potion.' Joan handed the man a small bottle containing purple liquid. 'Then wear the crystal around your neck and do not take it off, even when you are sleeping, even when you are making the beast with two backs, for at least one year. Each year, repeat the ceremony.'

The man took the crystal and the bottle from Joan's hand and put them in his pocket, handing her a pouch in exchange. He said thank you to Joan, raised the hood of his cloak and started walking towards the stairs.

Henry panicked. It was not that Joan had ever said explicitly that he should not come into the apothecary while she had a client, he just knew instinctively that he should not. He also knew that a wealthy man like this one would not appreciate being seen seeking out a witch, hence why he had left his horse in the street unguarded, without even an attendant to watch over it.

The man drew closer to the staircase but Henry could not make out his features beneath the shadow cast by his hood. Henry skipped up a few steps and hurried back into a crevice in the wall, hoping that the man would not notice him in the relative darkness of the stairwell. He held his breath as he heard the footsteps approaching. Henry could not understand why he felt so scared. What exactly did he think the man would do if he found him?

The sound of feet got closer. He closed his eyes, as if not being able to see would somehow make him less visible. The footsteps passed by him and continued up the stairs without breaking stride. Even though his eyes were closed, Henry felt the light outside stream down the stairwell as the door opened and then disappear again when the door closed.

Henry let out his breath and walked down the stairs to find

Joan still sitting at the desk – now reading a book.

'I sensed you were there, Henry,' Joan said before Henry had even fully entered the room. 'One day, I will teach you to hide your aura so you don't make such a racket.' Joan glanced up from her book and smiled at Henry. From the look on her face he could tell that Agnes had not been down here yet.

'A delivery is due,' Joan said as she got up and hugged Henry.

Henry tried to imagine what might be contained within this latest package.

'What's wrong?' Joan asked.

'I'm fine,' Henry lied as he sat on the spare seat by Joan's desk. 'Can't wait. I wonder what he'll bring.'

'Me too.' Joan smiled an uneasy smile at Henry and sat back in her seat.

There was a knock at the door. Joan looked to Henry as if she expected him to answer, but Henry did not know whether it was the delivery or Agnes, so he stayed in his chair.

'What you waiting for?' asked Joan. 'You can't seriously be expecting this old biddy to run up those stairs when fit legs is around now, can ya?'

Henry stood and walked up the stairs, his nerves creating a sickly taste in his mouth, and then he remembered that Agnes would never knock, because she had a key.

He got to the top of the stairs and shouted, 'Who is it?' without opening the door, just to be safe.

'I am a seeker but I come bearing gifts,' the man on the other side replied.

Henry opened the door, looked up and down the street and gestured for the man to enter. He wore a large cloak of fine quality and Henry noticed a metal breastplate visible underneath his lime-green tunic. He was probably moderately wealthy but certainly not a noble. Clearly he was a man that was prepared to fight. He had long, thick black hair, a stubbly beard that ran right up to his cheekbones, an olive complexion, skin that bore many scars and striking bright-green eyes. Henry wondered what things those bright eyes might have seen, but did not ask the guest anything. He sensed from the man's aura that questions would not be welcome.

Joan was still sitting at the table when they entered the room, but she quickly got up and hugged the guest with the same warmth with which she hugged Henry. He felt petty for noticing, and wondered what their history might be.

'Greetings, noble Vadoma,' the stranger said.

Henry had almost forgotten Joan's Gypsy name. It had been so many years since he had heard it.

'Greetings, Leander,' Joan replied and Leander kissed her on both cheeks. 'What does your order bring for us today?'

Leander raised the leather strap of his satchel over his head and placed the bag on the table. He opened the front flap and started to take out books, one by one. 'This is from India, by a sage called Ashvaghosha. It deals with the life of one they call the Buddha.' He placed the book on the table, looking very pleased with himself. 'This one, written in Arabic, comes from a place beyond the great sands called

Timbuktu and deals with the history of the kings and kingdoms of that region.' He laid the book next to the first. 'This one is in Latin, entitled *Epistulae Morales ad Lucilium* and written by a sage named Seneca.' He placed the third book on the table and so he continued until his satchel was empty. 'Eight books in total,' Leander stated, summing up his merchandise.

Butterflies tickled Henry's stomach at the thought of all the potential secrets contained in these texts. By the look on her face, Joan felt the same.

'This may well be the best delivery your order has ever brought us, Leander. Do let them know that it will not be forgotten,' Joan said.

'I just aim to serve, noble Vadoma,' Leander replied. 'I have no idea how you are going to translate all of it, but such things are none of my business.'

Henry and Joan exchanged a glance and only just managed to conceal their cheeky smiles.

'Indeed,' Joan said, 'you just keep encouraging them to bring me what they can any time one of you ventures into these waters. I will have the translations ready.' She walked over to a cupboard and took out three medium-sized bottles, each with a different-coloured potion in it. She handed them to Leander. 'These will be stronger than the last batch, so use them sparingly and wisely.'

'Yes, noble Vadoma,' Leander said as he carefully packed the vials into his satchel. 'We know well the power of your medicine and respect its dangers.'

Joan opened her desk drawer, lifted out a pile of books and handed them to Leander. 'The last set of translations.'

Leander placed the books into his satchel and bowed. 'If you will excuse me, I have some other business to attend to today and my ship leaves in a few hours.'

'Henry, show Leander out, please,' Joan said.

Henry and Leander walked back up the stairs. Henry let him out, looking up and down the street to check for Agnes as Leander walked away. Henry closed the door, double-locked it and ran down the stairs, almost falling over himself to get to the new books.

Joan had already gone through into the other room where she stored her books and the bases for making her medicines. She had all eight of the books spread out in front of her.

'Time to get to work, youngster,' she said to Henry affectionately. 'Which do you want to start with?'

Henry surveyed the covers. They were all made of plain brown leather but the shades of brown and types of design varied quite a bit. Henry was drawn to one in particular. It had the faint outline of a curved sword embossed on the cover and its leather was slightly darker than the others. 'This one first.' Henry pointed at the book that had come from beyond the sands and picked it up. He and Joan walked to the back of the room methodically, and then, as if on cue, faced the wall together and chanted an incantation.

Know thyself. To seek eternal wisdom
Look within to the only true kingdom
As above so below, as within, out.
The first thing a seeker must overcome?
Doubt

Henry's skin prickled with excitement. After the third utterance of the invocation a door shimmered into existence where only blank wall had stood a second ago. The door opened itself to them slowly, silently. Henry walked through first and Joan followed.

Henry always found the dim golden light emanating from the room behind the door instantly comforting. He found the geometric patterns on the few small hanging rugs mesmerising; there was no doubt in his mind that they contained some kind of mathematical wisdom. He found the energy in this room so magical that the intensity of his own gift was greatly amplified.

Henry sat on one of the straw mats in front of the log that served as a desk and placed the text on it. Joan sat down at the other end of the room and closed her eyes. They had figured out some time ago that Henry's gifts could be enhanced if Joan sent Henry energy while he worked. It also gave Joan some insight into his powers, though as hard as she tried and as powerful as she was in other ways, she could never replicate Henry's gifts herself – just as he could never do *chi* magic despite trying many times.

Henry picked up a quill from the inkwell, opened the first page and started studying the letters of the Arabic alphabet. But the language written here was not Arabic – even though the letters were. Henry closed his eyes, placed his left hand over the book and breathed deeply. Again the letters became colours, shapes, sounds and musical notes. Always a different pattern emerged and it was endlessly beautiful; it was the sun and the stars merged with mountains and oceans, explosions of triple blackness, splashes of purple, floods of red and orange and the finest song of instruments Henry had never heard. Letters carved themselves out of these patterns and became full words that Henry could read. His right hand furiously copied out the book's contents, writing at a speed that no one in a normal state could ever achieve.

Henry was away in a trance now, not conscious of the process, his gift in full control of his being. He turned the pages of the text with one hand and wrote with the other, each page taking just a few seconds to copy.

Within the colours and patterns Henry saw visions of armies clashing. A lone soldier was aflame, fighting to rescue his daughter from amid the ruins of a burned-out palace. The palace, forged from melted bronze, gold and ivory fell back into the hungry sun of Henry's visions. The father and daughter fled across an ocean of great sand mountains that opened themselves up and collapsed into the sky. A ship of stardust and soil carried the father and daughter – both of them still bright like human flames – to a new palace formed of stone and cold air. Henry fought to keep hold of these visions from the text but as soon as he left this state he would remember nothing he had seen, read or felt. The flame that was the soldier faded until it was nothing.

Henry reached the last page, closed the book and he was jerked from his alternate state of consciousness. The aftershocks always felt harder the longer he had stayed in the state, and it seemed that the more pleasurable the vision had been, the sharper the sting. Henry felt himself flinch before he returned to normal. He smiled at Joan and they walked back up to the wall and chanted.

Doubt
The first thing a seeker must overcome?
As above so below, as within, out.
Look within to the only true kingdom
Know thyself. To seek eternal wisdom

The door reappeared, glowing like the gold stitching on the dress of that pretty woman on the roof of St Paul's. Henry wondered if she'd laugh him off so easily if she could see his powers. They walked back into the library.

'How many more can you do today?' Joan asked.

'Noble Vadoma,' Henry said in a half-mocking voice, 'I am at your service.'

Joan gave Henry an affectionate push in the shoulder. 'Which one shall we do next?'

Henry, put his hand over the books and picked a Latin text called *Meditations*. 'This one.'

As he picked up the book, Henry heard the front door burst open. The sounds of two sets of angry feet came trouncing down the stairs. Henry felt the taste of dread, yet he had no choice but to go out into the main room of the apothecary with Joan.

'You little rascal! Look what you did to my boy,' Agnes yelled, and lunged forward to grab Henry.

Before Agnes reached Henry, Joan closed her eyes and grunted, sending a shot of pure *chi* energy that pushed Agnes back.

'Let's talk about this,' Joan said.

'Talk about what?' Agnes demanded as she gestured to Matthew's face. Agnes lurched forward again and Joan sent another shot of *chi* to knock her back.

'Henry, did you do this?' Joan asked.

'Ay, course he did,' Matthew said from behind his mother.

Henry stayed silent.

'Why?' Joan asked.

Henry wanted to speak. He wanted to tell Joan about his awful day and how Matthew insulting his mother was just the final straw, but instead he went silent. He could feel the moody look on his face, which always took over at times like this.

Agnes went for Henry again and Joan pushed her back with *chi*. Agnes thudded into the tree. She groaned and shot *chi* back at Joan, knocking her into the desk and sending potions spilling all over the place. Henry knew it was about to get serious, so he slid under the desk. Agnes could never match the strength of Joan's *chi* magic. He almost laughed as he saw Matthew scramble back up the stairs to get out of the way too.

Joan let out a strange guttural roar while squeezing the crystal around her neck, her power taking hold of her sister's body. Agnes froze as if a pole had been thrust through her. Unable to move, she winced, her eyes moving frantically in their sockets.

'Joan . . . stop.' Agnes could barely get the words out as the force choked her breath.

Joan squeezed her crystal once more, and Agnes crumbled, hitting the floor hard. When Agnes had regained her breath and composure, she got up, glaring at Henry, who still sat under the table flinching, scared the energy might hit him.

'Listen here, you little runt. Your "auntie" Joan will not always be there to protect you and I think you know that already.'

Agnes stormed back up the stairs. Matthew waited for his mother to pass him and then followed. The door slammed so hard that the branches on the tree shook. Henry knew Agnes would make good on her threat eventually – Joan had only saved him temporarily.

Joan paused, as if waiting for Agnes and Matthew to be out of earshot, then said, 'Henry, you really have to control your temper.' Her sternness gave her face a mean quality that reminded Henry of Agnes – the way her eyes narrowed and her lip curled up to the left.

Henry could not speak.

'Well, don't you have anything to say for yourself?'

Henry wanted to explain himself and the frustration of not being able to find the words just made him even angrier.

'Oh, so you want to do the silent routine? Then no more translating for today. Go and entertain yourself.'

As Joan looked at him, he could tell she was seeing attitude where really he felt relief that he had not been cursed and gratitude to Joan for protecting him.

'No, that's too easy. You are going to copy out lines by hand – no using your gift – and write "I must control my temper" five thousand times.'

Henry sat down at the desk obediently, while Joan grabbed some paper and dumped it in front of him. 'Seeing as you are looking so cocky about it, let's call it ten thousand times.'

Henry started writing, fighting to contain his irritation, while Joan stormed back over to her desk. An hour passed and then another. Henry continued copying out his lines, but inside he was fuming now, bored and frustrated. He was annoyed with Joan and he thought about his own mother, how he wished he'd grown up with her instead of this witch that he was not even related to. Henry hated himself for thinking it. Among all of the other things she'd done for him, that witch had literally saved his life. One summer, when Henry was a small boy, he had jumped into the Thames because some older boys had dared him to. He remembered grasping at air and getting nothing but a throatful of filthy water, and the feeling of fire in his muscles as he battled against the river and his lungs gave up, the pain in his head like getting pricked by a thousand pins at once. The face of the person that pulled him out of the water and up to the riverbank belonged to the old witch sat across the room from him now. The person that helped him overcome his fears and then taught him to swim was that same old witch. Joan looked over at Henry periodically and he could sense her guilt, making him feel even worse.

Finally Joan came to sit next to Henry. She put her arm around him and said in a soft voice, 'You really need to control your temper, Henry.'

At her touch, Henry let out his tears, crying uncontrollably as he turned into Joan's chest. She hugged him hard.

'Ay, I know,' he said through his sobs.

As they travel, moon after violent moon, the general shows his daughter many things: the fighting arts, the healing arts, the art of magic.

6

Joan hugged him tighter and tighter, and eventually Henry calmed down, able to take a deep, controlled breath. He smelled lavender and rose – Joan's hair. Henry could not help but smell it a few more times before he caught himself and pulled away.

He felt Joan hold on to him gently, but this only made him move away more firmly. She let go with a reluctant, lingering touch.

They looked at each other for a moment.

'Come on, let's get some fresh air,' Joan suggested.

Henry nodded.

The river was a little quieter than usual but still many small boats and big ships jostled along the water. Henry squinted as he tried to watch a flock of birds crossing the path of the fading sun. It made him think about one of his sonnets:

The birds can just fly . . . they don't even try

He thought about it some more. *Nah, that's cheesy.*

The birds can fly and they don't even practise

Too many syllables.

The birds can just fly . . . they don't even think

Better. Another line came quickly:

Don't drop from the sky nor crash their fine tails

Henry looked down and focused on the ships on the water.

Ships crash and burn

'Burn' there is too clichéd . . . he thought. He looked at Joan then back to the water. She was leaving him alone, sensing he was in his own thoughts. His mind returned to the ships.

Ships crash and capsize

The two c sounds go well together.

Ships crash and capsize, they burn and they sink

Nice.

Henry remembered going down to the shipyard as a boy and watching the men building the ships. He had always been amazed at how trees could be turned into floating castles.

Henry began mumbling the whole of his evolving sonnet to himself.

The bird and the ship, the ship and the bird
One that is free because of its nature
The bird and the ship, the ship and the bird
One is man-made, thus destined to failure
The birds can just fly, they don't even think
Don't drop from the sky nor crash their fine tails
Ships crash and capsize, they burn and they sink
Just a few trees held together by nails

He'd dreamed of sailing off in a ship to the faraway lands he had read about. He'd pictured tropical fruits and year-round sunshine, mischievous dwarves and magical fairies. The faraway lands had seemed like a great getaway from all of his troubles, from the stink of Romeville, the curses of Agnes, the hunger, the dirt and the disrespect. *I'll go one day*, he'd said to himself. *I'll leave this godforsaken place once and for all.*

Then other images had come to him – men with dogs' heads, fire-breathing dragons and huge cats that ran as fast as horses and hunted people in the lands far away.

Maybe Romeville is not so bad after all, he thought.

'I'm sorry,' Joan said, breaking the silence between them, and Henry became conscious of just how loud the streets were, filled with the hum of people. Henry walked a little faster. He noticed Joan struggling to keep up, yet he did not slow down.

'I'm sorry, Henry, for everything,' she repeated louder, almost shouting after him.

Again Henry did not speak.

'Henry?' she called, louder still.

Henry did not want Joan to shout after him – he hated attracting attention to himself in public – so he stopped by a small section of wall that served as a good viewing point to look out over the water. He wondered about the kinds of ships his mother had travelled on and where she might be now.

'Sorry that I am black or sorry that I am an orphan?' Henry asked Joan without taking his eyes off the water.

'You know that's not what I mean,' Joan replied. 'And we don't know that your parents have gone over.'

Henry started walking again, slowly this time, and Joan followed. They weaved through a crowded section of pavement until they came to a less busy area and Henry continued, 'They may as well be dead.' He chucked the words across the air at Joan with a whip of his head.

'Don't speak such tilly-vally,' Joan barked back, the anger tightening her lips and eyes.

'It's not nonsense – they are dead to me.'

'Don't say that!' Joan was almost shouting now.

Henry put his hand up towards Joan as if it could block her words. He was about to say something smug until he remembered that Joan's mother had been burned at the stake in

80

front of her when Joan was a child, accused of witchcraft. The main reason Joan and Agnes had fled to England from Germany was because of the persecution of witches and Gypsies there. No wonder Joan got angry when he said his parents were dead so flippantly. Henry went quiet.

They walked down the hill towards the big fishmongers, passing several homeless vagabonds lying on the ground, and leaned against the small stone wall that prevented people falling over the hill on to the riverbank. Henry wondered how long before the beadle arrested them for being homeless and moved them on to another parish. Street children begged affluent-looking passers-by but did not seem to notice Henry and Joan.

'One of the few benefits of being poor, eh,' Henry said.

'What is?' Joan asked.

'They don't bother you.' Henry gestured to the begging children. 'And you ain't gotta worry about getting robbed either 'cos everyone knows you ain't got nothing.'

'Forsooth,' Joan said and they both laughed.

Henry looked into the faces of the begging children and tried to imagine what had happened to them and their parents. One brown-haired boy with a surprisingly happy face was missing an arm. A girl who could not have been more than six had skin worn so hard it made her look elderly and a crouched-over posture caused by poorly developed bones. A boy of about ten was missing his right eye.

Henry remembered what had happened to the street children who were not good enough at stealing at the thieves' school –

pinned down by some faceless adult to have an eye gouged out or a limb cut off so that they would make better beggars.

Maybe thieving is not so noble after all, Henry thought. He looked to Joan and back to the children. His fate could have been so much worse and he had Joan to thank that it wasn't.

They reached the bottom of the hill, holding their noses as they passed the fishmongers, both laughing as they noticed the other doing the same. The swarms of flies surrounding the fish guts always made Henry feel slightly queasy.

'Sorry,' Henry said.

'Nay bother,' Joan replied and her tone told Henry she had really understood his sorry. 'I'm sure your mother is still alive and I'll bet she thinks about you every day.'

Henry tried to picture the image of his mother that came to him in his dreams but failed. He looked around for things to distract him.

London had a beautiful mood about it at this time of day during these rare hot summers. The sun had disappeared but there was still some orange light in the sky and people were scurrying about to get their last few errands done before the end of the day.

Henry watched lawyers and judges emerging from the inns of court and flooding into the more upmarket alehouses for their evening drinks. He wondered how many common folk they had condemned to death today. He thought up the starting lines of a sonnet about death and the injustice of Romeville and muttered them to himself.

Death to the poor man; sport of the gentry
Justice? What justice, if you cannot pay?
Steal as you like so long as it's plenty
Take for your hunger and death ends your day . . .

'You know why I say my mum is dead, Auntie Joan?' Henry asked waiting for her to reply. ''Cos what if she is alive and well and she just doesn't care about me?'

Joan went to speak but paused as if she had thought better of it. Henry imagined his mother enjoying her life somewhere beautiful, with a new family – without a thought about what had happened to him. It made him feel sick.

'I'm sure that's not true,' Joan said finally.

'But how do you know?'

'I just do.'

'I've seen her, you know,' Henry said.

'What?' Joan asked.

'I have seen parts of her life in my dreams. I can't figure out if it's 'cos you have told me the stories so many times, but I've seen my grandpa and his battles, the death of my grandma, my mum's journey across the sands – all of it.'

'Why didn't you mention it before?'

'People have dreams,' Henry shrugged, changing direction towards the indoor market. 'Tell me about her,' Henry demanded.

'As you said, I have told you many times.'

'I know the tale of her life. But what was she like . . . as a person?'

Joan's eyes rolled upwards the way they always did when she was trying to recall a memory. 'She was different. She was not a pauper like us. Yeah, she lived with me and Agnes and we were poor together, but she weren't scared of wealthy people like we were.' Warmth flooded Henry as he noticed a new brightness in Joan. 'I think she must have come from some kind of gentlefolk back in Benin, even though she denied it when I asked. Her dad was a general after all.'

Henry looked at the market-stall traders packing up their stalls after a hard day's work, then around at the London poor. These were the only people he'd ever known. *My own mother, an aristocrat? Nay.*

'What else?' Henry asked.

'She was the life and soul of the party. She loved wine and music. She was a great dancer and an even better singer. She played the lute and the harp very well. Clearly those gifts skipped over you.'

'Forsooth,' Henry replied and they both laughed.

'But you got her gift of reading.'

'True.' Henry said as he imagined his mother reading a huge tome and felt a pinch of pride that the rare gift ran in his family.

They emerged from the other end of the market and walked down to the water's edge. Henry took off his rotten cloth shoes and let the ripples wash over his feet but Joan stayed a yard or two behind him, just out of the water's reach.

'But she also had a sorrow in her eyes that never left,' Joan said. 'She had already lost her whole family and she knew as soon as she got pregnant with you that she would have to give you up, that you could not have been easy—'

'She did not *have* to give me up, Auntie Joan,' Henry cut in.

Joan paused. 'I know curses might seem like a strange thing to normal people, but if you knew what I knew you'd see how real they are.'

Henry huffed and carried on staring out at the water.

'Your mother was a charming woman too, like me and Agnes,' Joan continued. 'Only, she used her gifts for good – as I try to, unlike my sister.'

At the mention of Agnes, Henry turned to look to Joan. 'Why is Agnes like that?' Henry could see Joan really thinking before she answered.

''Cos the arts are neither good nor bad, but tools that can be used. Some people come here from the spirit realm and are just drawn to destruction, or things happen to them in life that fashion them that way, like Agnes. Your ma and me, we are healers. But that's a very painful thing too.'

'Why?'

'Because you have to carry the pain of so many others on top of your own. Your ma walked with that pain, with the dark curse that was placed on your family, her whole life. She was a remarkable woman, considering.'

Henry swallowed hard and curled his mouth, stretching his face in any way he could that would distract him from his emotions. He picked up a stone and threw it into the water, counting the skims. Then another stone and another, while Joan watched him.

Henry had just noticed how dark it was getting when Joan spoke.

'Shall we go back?'

Henry took it more as a statement than a question and they turned to walk back through the market, up the hill and towards the slum.

Men carrying flaming torches ignited the street lights as London's sky darkened. It had been a tough day and Henry just wanted to sleep. He hoped that tomorrow would be better.

Henry felt the dream descending, slowly weighing on the brain space behind his eyelids. His mother's image emerged from purple silk and even through the dream he wondered what, if anything, that meant. The little boy at the well laughed a rancid high-pitched laugh and his teeth fell out on the floor by the well head. Henry was sucked through the dark gap in the boy's mouth to the baker's Adam's apple pulsing in a jar of one of Joan's solutions, while Henry's mother somehow watched.

Do I as a Devil seem? *she asked Henry without speaking.*

Then why do you giveth them power? *she said, as if she had heard Henry's response.*

They hunt elephant, zebra and wildebeest, even the mighty leopard they kill. The young girl is becoming a warrior, like her father, the general.

7

The monkey came out on horseback and the crowd's laughter shook the arena. Henry chuckled too, despite his unease that the monkey would be dead soon.

'Why are they booing the monkey?' Henry said, not really expecting Mary to know the answer, as the crowd's laughter turned to jeers.

"Cos it's clothed like a Spaniard, obviously,' Mary shouted over the crowd's noise. Henry looked harder and saw the pointed helmet, extra baggy breeches and flashes of yellow all over that typified a Spaniard.

'See, you know not everything after all,' Mary added with a smile. Henry gave a friendly shrug and joined in, wondering how they'd taught a monkey to ride a horse in the first place.

A masked man emerged from the stables into the arena holding the leashes of five large grey mastiffs. The dogs barked and drooled, pulling away from the leashes to get at the horse. The crowd erupted with roars and claps, shouts and stamps; the air smelled of beer, bread and sweat.

'Here we go,' Mary shouted.

The masked man bent down and unclipped the first of the dogs. The mastiff sprinted off towards the horse as if propelled by a cannon. The audience's stamps and claps grew ever louder;

a row of drummers started beating their large round drums slowly, menacingly. The masked man let another dog free of its leash and it too sped off.

Henry tried to follow it with his eyes, but was distracted by a figure weaving his way through the crowd towards them. It took him a moment to register that it was Matthew.

'Did you tell that knave brother of yours that we would be here?' Henry shouted to Mary.

'What?' Mary yelled back.

'Did you tell Matthew we would be here? That's why you insisted we stay by the pie stand, isn't it?'

'What? Pardon? My ears can't hear you.' Mary smiled at Henry with her eyebrows raised.

Matthew pushed past the two people in front of them and hugged Mary. He nodded at Henry and Henry returned the gesture, suppressing a sting of guilt as he looked at Matthew's bruised face. Matthew stood next to Mary and turned back to face the action as the first dog jumped at the horse and bounced off, easily brushed aside by the speed and power of the horse's gallop. The masked man unclipped the remaining three dogs so all five began chasing the horse and the monkey around the arena, paws and hooves kicking up moving clouds of dust.

'Get it!' Matthew shouted, egging the dogs on.

The sun shone through the dust, reflecting off the horse's coat, giving the scene a beautiful quality that reminded Henry of the Italian paintings he saw in church. The dogs jumped at the horse one after the other but each bounced off the horse's strong legs and body, leaving only scratches.

After each dog had tried this several times without success, the dogs just stopped.

'Get that foreigner!' Matthew shouted.

Henry spun to look at Matthew. The word 'foreigner' stung, making him think of the mob at the bakers, and the vandalised Dutch church.

'Get that *Spanish* monkey,' Matthew said as if correcting himself.

Henry looked into the eyes of the dogs, and saw an intelligence that he'd never imagined. *The dogs are thinking*, Henry said to himself.

Sure enough, the dogs started moving again. But they were not charging after the horse in one line as they had been doing before. Instead, they each shot off in a different direction, creating a formation that surrounded the horse so they could close in and the horse would have nowhere to go.

Now the horse stopped, as if it had realised what was happening, and it bucked in fear. If the monkey had not been strapped to the saddle it may well have dropped out.

'The horse is quick mettled. He knows what's coming!' Henry shouted to Mary.

'Yeah, but quick mettle can't save him,' Matthew said.

'Quick mettle and quick valour can though,' Henry retorted.

'Get that prancer! Come on, ye dogs,' Matthew shouted into the air as if he had not heard Henry's remark.

The dogs charged towards the horse, closing in on it from

every direction. The horse started galloping again, but the dogs got closer and closer – just a few feet away now. Mary grabbed Henry's arm in excitement as she stood on tiptoe to get the best possible view over the heads of the men in front of her.

Henry saw fear in the eyes of the horse as one of the mastiffs charged at its front and leaped up at the horse's exposed neck. The horse jumped, colliding with the dog in the air, the clash cracking bone inside the dog and sending it flying. The horse trampled over the whimpering dog's body.

'Mettle and valour,' Henry repeated and Mary gave him the side-eye, to let him know how childish he was being.

But the jump had slowed the horse's momentum and the other four dogs caught up and leaped at the horse – two on its right side, one on the left and one from behind. The dogs flew through the air, their mouths wide open, their sharpened teeth exposed, and landed on the horse like darts, each sinking teeth into flesh.

'*Bene, bene!*' Matthew screamed, repeatedly tapping Mary on the back with his large palm.

The crowd bellowed its loudest roar. *The horse knows it's about to be killed*, Henry thought.

'Come on, ye dogs,' Matthew shouted again.

The horse bucked over and over again, trying to force the dogs' teeth out of its flesh. It managed to throw off the one behind and the two on its right side, but the dog on the left just would not fall off, no matter how hard the horse bucked.

'Look how stout that dog is,' Matthew said to Mary, but

Henry knew it was to him really. Mary was concentrating on the action, gripping their arms either side of her, ignoring their tit-for-tat comments.

Henry closed his eyes and prayed quickly. *Dear Lord Jesus, please let this horse and monkey survive and kill these wretched dogs.*

He opened his eyes just in time to see the other three dogs jumping back on to the horse, digging their teeth even deeper than before. The horse made an awful guttural sound that twisted Henry's nerves as the drumming became a fast, furious march. Just when Henry thought the audience could not get any louder, they did. Matthew seemed to be the loudest of all, yelping with joy, as happy as if he were eating a steak.

I did my best, Henry thought, looking at the horse. *I even prayed for you, big fella.*

The horse jerked and turned but its movements had nowhere near the force of a few moments ago. The four dogs still hung from its body, growling through their clenched jaws.

Henry felt Matthew looking over in his direction, trying to share the excitement of the moment by making eye contact. Henry deliberately kept his eyes on the action.

The horse swayed like a drunken man, no longer making any noises.

Boom! It fell to its left and collapsed with a thud, instantly crushing the very dog that had sealed its fate in a kind of poetic justice.

Well done, big fella, at least you took two of them with you.

'The dog is officially kissed off,' Henry announced.

'Yeah, but the horse is dead too,' Matthew shot back.

'Sometimes you gotta go out like a proper vagabond, even if you die,' Henry said.

'Nay, better to stay alive by whatever means. Reckless valour ain't no good for anyone,' Matthew said.

'Better than being a coward,' Henry replied.

'Oh my God! Will you two old autem-morts just stop your nattering and enjoy the show?' Mary shouted, shaking her head quickly like she was trying to rid it of fleas. Both of the boys went quiet.

The monkey lay there unharmed. The crowd started to boo again. 'Get the monkey, get the monkey, kill the Spanish foe!' The chant started low at first but soon the whole audience had joined in, including Mary and Matthew.

'Get the monkey, get the monkey, kill the Spanish foe,' they chanted joyfully, clapping to a rhythm as they spoke.

With the horse dead, Henry *really* wanted the monkey to survive. Fighting and killing between dogs and horses and bears and bulls seemed fair enough – they were all fierce animals that could fight back – but there was something wrong about killing a defenceless little monkey. Yet Henry joined in the chant, since he certainly did not want to appear as if he sympathised with Spanish Catholics. Though secretly he hoped the monkey would get away somehow.

The man in the mask walked back into the arena with a new dog on a leash. He poked a stake into the ground and tied the dog's leash to it. He walked slowly over towards the dead horse, waving showman-like to the crowd. He unstrapped the monkey and held it in the air with one hand, raising his other hand to signal for the audience to be quiet. To Henry's surprise, the whole arena fell deathly silent at once.

'This here is our Spanish foe,' the masked man shouted as he held the monkey aloft. 'It shall be crushed before the might of our queen and our country. Long live England. Long live Elizabeth.' The man threw the monkey high into the air across the arena, but it landed perfectly, like a cat.

'Long live England! Long Live Elizabeth,' the crowd chanted over and over as the masked man walked back to the new dog tied to the pole.

'There goes the dead prancer,' Matthew said, laughing as six attendants loaded the horse's corpse and the old dogs on to a cart.

'You trying to be funny, jolt-head?' Henry barked, turning his body to face Matthew.

'I'm just enjoying the show.' Matthew put his hands up defensively.

'Yeah, that's what I thought, knave,' Henry muttered.

Only the masked man, the fresh dog and the monkey were left on the floor of the arena. The crowd let out a cheer of excitement as the man unclipped the dog. But the dog did not chase after the monkey. Instead it ran over to where the horse had lain and started to lick up its blood. The masked man ran after it and kicked the dog from behind. The dog flew into the air, making Henry laugh so hard it hurt his ribs. He caught Matthew's eye as they laughed, and both quickly muted their smiles.

The dog would not move towards the monkey. The masked man kicked the dog again, but this only made the crowd's laughter change in tone. It was clear they were now laughing at the masked man and his impotent rage, not at the dog.

The masked man took out a dagger, walked up to the dog and stabbed it. The dog was killed instantly.

'There goes another dead dog,' Henry said, looking at Matthew provocatively.

Matthew just shrugged.

The masked man headed for the monkey again, making a show to the crowd. He went to pick it up but it bit his hand and ran. Everyone was almost crying with laughter now. The masked man chased after the monkey, but it was unusually fast and scurried up to the wall of the arena, scaling it and jumping into the crowd – just at the bottom of the tier in front of Henry.

Men trampled over one another, cups smashed and beers spilled as they fought to get to the monkey. Everyone wanted to be the one to kill the symbol of the Spanish foe. Men started punching each other and throwing things as the monkey disappeared into a sea of bodies. Soon the men just in front of Henry were fighting. One man fell backwards and bumped into Henry, almost knocking him over. Henry pushed him back hard, knocking the man into his friends.

'What you doing, Moor?' the man spat with rage, throwing his cup at Henry.

Henry managed to block his face and the cup bounced off his arms and away into the brawling crowd. The man charged back at Henry but did not see the wild punch coming from Matthew. It knocked him backwards again and the man was swallowed into the crowd as the brawl continued to spread.

Matthew smiled at Henry through his bruised eyes and Henry smiled back – a proper smile this time.

Trumpets sounded and some of the constable's men marched out into the centre of the arena, drawing their swords as if ready to charge at the crowd. The trumpets sounded again and the brawlers started to calm down. Moments later, order was restored, as if by magic.

A group of men held the monkey – now dead – aloft and shouted, 'Long live England! Long Live Elizabeth.' The crowd, including Mary and Matthew, joined in, but Henry stayed silent this time. After a few minutes the constable's men sheathed their swords and disappeared back into the tunnel from where they had come.

Henry looked at Matthew, wanting to say thank you, but instead he just nodded. Matthew nodded back.

'I'm gonna get a pie,' Mary said. 'Either of you want one?'

'I'll come with,' Henry said.

'Nay, it's only there,' Mary replied, pointing to the pie stall. 'Besides, you need to hold our spots here.'

Henry smiled – he knew what Mary was trying to do. 'Ay, I'll take a sausage pie.'

'Me too, please,' Matthew said.

Henry reached in his pocket to give Mary some money as Matthew went to do the same.

'I'll pay,' Henry said, trying to sound nonchalant.

Mary walked off. The drummers and trumpeters played while the arena floor was cleared for the main event.

'Nice shot back there,' Henry said, 'but you know I could have taken him.'

Matthew nodded and the two boys stood quietly for a few moments.

'I saw my chief prigger earlier,' Matthew announced.

'And?' Henry said.

'He has a big foist on the books.'

'What you telling me for?' Henry said.

'It's a duke's house.'

Henry noted the awe in Matthew's voice when he said the word 'duke', and himself felt that same yearning. Yes, he resented the wealthy because of their arrogance, because of the way they treated their servants and because they could basically get any poor person killed if they really wanted to. But Henry would still much rather be a rich man than a poor one.

'No servants or family – some kind of loner,' Matthew continued. 'He has one guard who goes with him everywhere. Every Wednesday evening, he spends time with a *night woman*.'

Henry smiled at the thought of sex. Matthew had already

lost his virginity – or so he told Henry – and so Henry had been pretending for a year or so now that he had lost his too. He was desperate for it to be true, and though he could easily just go to the stews, he really wanted to find a girl that he actually liked.

'So that's when we'll do it, if you agree of course?' Matthew said. Henry's little daydream about sex had almost caused him to forget what Matthew was talking about. Matthew leaned in and whispered in Henry's ear. 'The duke is said to have one of the best libraries in all of England.'

Henry tried to picture the duke's library, what it might look like and how many books it might have. *One of the best in England?* he thought, imagining the smell of the pages and the feel of the leather. The houses they usually robbed were those of the middling sort – small merchants or tailors, yeomen or tradesmen. Their homes were made of cheap wattle and daub, with few expensive possessions and certainly none of them had a library. A duke's mansion was a whole new category of risk . . . and potential reward.

Matthew carried on whispering in Henry's ear. 'All my prigger wants in exchange is one piece of jewellery – a golden bird that the duke keeps in a safe. So we'll need your lock-picking skills to get it out.'

The crowd erupted again as Sackerson, London's most famous bear, was brought out into the middle of the arena. Bets were placed and drinks and food were ordered as people prepared for the main event. Mary returned with the pies and handed one each to Henry and Matthew.

'Just think about it,' Matthew said to Henry.

'What's that?' Mary asked.

'Nothing,' Henry and Matthew said at the same time.

But it is said the general is cursed.

8

'But we are well hidden by the bushes, Henry,' Matthew assured him. 'If I pee here, he will never see me.'

'But you won't be ready to strike. Stop being a baby and hold it in.' Henry knew he was being petty but he enjoyed feeling like the boss.

'Look, just squeeze into that corner there.' Henry pointed to a natural gap in the bushes. 'Turn your back and make sure you don't pee on me,' he added.

'Thanks, boss,' Matthew said. He worked his way into the corner and let out a dramatic sigh.

Henry heard a faint scrambling in the bushes.

'Can you hear that?' he asked Matthew.

'Hear what?' Matthew replied.

'Be quiet and listen . . .'

Henry watched the bushes as the noise seemed to get closer.

'Get your cuttle-bung ready,' Henry commanded, drawing his own knife. The bushes moved again.

'Hey foisters.' Mary emerged into the clearing where the boys were hidden.

'What the hell are you doing here?' Matthew demanded, still peeing. 'Go back home, now!'

'So I am good enough to help you with petty pickpocketing,

but I can't be involved in proper foists?'

Matthew finished and turned back towards where Henry and Mary were.

'That's right, this is big boy stuff, now go home,' Matthew commanded.

'Shh,' Henry said to Matthew. 'She's here now, so we don't have a choice. We could probably use an extra pair of hands for a house *that* big.'

'I am serious, she needs to go home. This ain't for little girls.'

'Well, the fact she followed us here without either of us clocking her means she probably *is* ready,' Henry said.

Mary smiled mockingly at her brother.

The front door opened. Henry's heart rate quickened.

A man emerged and closed the door behind him. His face was weathered and his hair was fully grey, yet he had an athletic physique rather than the usual plump roundness that older men of means tended to have – their stomachs fat from a lifetime of feasting. The man was not surrounded by servants as most noblemen were, but he had that smug look that told Henry that this was, indeed, the duke. The duke looked strong and proud, like a soldier. He had a large nose and bird-like eyes, small and sharp, and his unusually thick eyebrows were the only funny feature on an otherwise very serious-looking face. *He looks like a brandy drinker*, Henry thought. From all his years hanging around pubs, Henry had noticed that men's looks always corresponded to their drink of choice. He did not know exactly what it was he was looking for, but he could always tell a brandy man from a wine drinker or a man who loved beer – though everybody drank beer of course.

A large man appeared from behind the house, pulling two horses by the reins. This man did not look smug, but hard as nails, even from Henry's distance. He held one horse steady as the duke jumped up into the saddle and then mounted the other horse himself. They galloped off, their silhouettes swallowed by the night.

'Time to mill a ken,' Mary said eagerly and she went to move. Henry put his arm up to stop her.

'Let's wait 'til we know the duke is far away and not about to turn back 'cos he forgot something, eager beaver.'

'Oh yes, I forgot I am working with a trained pro, the world-renowned Public Foister, Henry of the Billingsgate school,' Mary said in her best ceremonial voice.

'Forsooth,' Henry replied and thumped his chest three times.

'When you two have quite finished kissing up to each other, we have a house to rob,' Matthew said.

Henry went silent and watched the house as intently as before, as if he were still waiting for the duke to come out. Ten minutes passed, then fifteen.

'All right, move your stamps,' Henry said, deciding that they had waited long enough. He fought his way out of the dense bushes, followed by Matthew and Mary, catching a mouthful of leaf and the occasional slap of a twig.

Henry ran towards the front door, taking in the house as if he were seeing it for the first time. It was three storeys tall and almost as wide as Henry's entire street, made from polished limestone that shone even in near darkness. A large water fountain made of sculptures of winged children stood in front of the house. Henry enjoyed the sound of running water mixed with the faint echoes of their feet as they scurried across the pebblestones covering the huge courtyard. *How much did all these stones cost?* Henry wondered.

At the door, Henry took his wires and a small mechanical contraption out of his sack. Graham had left him alone for half a day two summers ago and Henry had used that time to make a lock-picking device like the ones he had seen Moll use. He knew Graham would go crazy if he found out. *Stealing kept me from starving*, Henry repeated to himself, feeling guilty.

He fiddled with the locks on the front door. First one, then the second, and finally the third lock popped open with ease.

'Behold my skills,' Henry said, nodding and patting his chest before leading the way into the house.

He froze for a moment, and Matthew almost bumped into him. Henry had robbed many houses before, but none such as this. Everything about this house screamed of outrageous wealth. At the front was a large open room that seemed more like a banqueting hall to Henry. A winding staircase in the middle curved up to a beautiful balcony that reminded him of the expensive seats at the theatre. The sweet smell of beeswax candles filled the air, not the horrible odour of tallow candles that poor people burned. There was a large wooden clock and even an animal-fur rug on the floor. Henry knew that most wealthy people hung their rugs as displays. So how rich would someone have to be to put a rug *on the floor?*

Every detail in the house seemed carved to perfection, making it more like a work of art than a home. Henry wondered how the duke could possibly keep this place so immaculately clean without servants. *Does the duke clean things himself?* Henry almost laughed out loud at the absurdity of the idea.

Henry and Matthew each pulled a large cloth bag from their breeches. 'Matthew, you take the ground floor,' Henry said. 'Mary and I will go upstairs. Mary, you take whatever other rooms you find. I'll take the master's room and the study. I'll whistle when it's time to leave, so listen out for it.'

'Mary doesn't have a bag, she should stay down here with me,' Matthew said.

Mary pulled a bag from under her shirt.

'A good foister always comes prepared,' she said, thumping her chest like Henry had.

'She should still stay down here with me. Little girls need all the help they can get.'

'Stop being a jolt-head,' Henry said, gesturing to Mary that it was time to move.

'Remember to get the thing in the safe,' Matthew called, as Henry and Mary raced up the stairs.

Henry strode into the master's room and went straight for the safe at the back of the wardrobe, exactly where Matthew's prigger had said it would be. The lock was quite different from any Henry had seen before and it took him much longer than he would have liked to open it, but he got there eventually.

Henry reached inside and felt an object wrapped in a velvet pouch. He took it out of the safe and removed the object from the pouch. Its beauty made Henry laugh out loud with delight. It was a small statue of a bird, made from solid gold and encrusted with precious stones. It had a cute puffy stomach and a small pointed beak. If Henry had to guess which bird it was, he would have said it was a finch.

It was easily the finest item Henry had ever laid his hands on. The details seemed more like the work of magicians than goldsmiths – every barb on every feather visible, the tiny eyeballs with gemstone pupils. Henry could not imagine how much it would be worth. Two lines for his sonnet came to him as he stared at the golden bird:

The Bird, the Ship, what's freedom and meaning
Our ships move only with wind or labour

Henry tried to think of a couplet to match the two lines but they would not come. He put the gold bird in its pouch and placed it in a secret pocket he had sewn inside his breeches.

It was now time for Henry to steal for himself. He looked through drawers and cupboards and searched for hidden compartments. He examined every item he picked up, quickly but thoroughly, considering how much he might fetch for the piece and how many days' food that would translate to. He judged this against the size, shape and weight of the item and then cast aside what did not pass his secret equation. Once he'd finished with the master's room he was sure he'd acquired his greatest prize yet, even though his sack was only half-full.

He moved on . . . and found the library.

The duke's library was beyond what Henry ever imagined he would get to see, let alone take from: hundreds of books all neatly arranged in rows along the walls, going so far up towards the ceiling that there was a long ladder for anyone who needed to reach the high shelves. Some of the books were in a special glass cabinet and he figured that these must be the most expensive ones.

He walked towards the cabinet, but could not help getting distracted and wishing he could steal everything. *So much knowledge, so many stories.* Henry knew he would never have a library like this – and that even if by some miracle he ever did, he'd never live long enough to properly read all the books within it. The thought depressed him.

The key was still in the door of the glass cabinet, so he opened it and started to scan the titles. He took a pile of books from the shelf and looked over them, trying to decide which ones to steal. Two of the books had types of writing Henry had never seen before. He studied the beauty of the symbols for a moment and then closed his eyes to tune into his gift to decipher them.

大央公畫央記 'The Records of the Grand Historian by Sima Quan.' Henry mumbled the title to himself.

Something told him this one might come from the land of

Cathay that he had read about in the travels of Marco Polo.

The writing on the next book was just as strange, though less beautiful.

gɪlgəmɛʃ/ 'The Epic of Gilgamesh,' Henry said out loud again.

The next three that drew his attention were all in familiar languages.

Πολιτεία – *The Republic*

Livres des Merveilles du Monde – Book of the Marvels of the World

Anabasis Alexandri – Alexander's Journey Up Country from the Sea

Henry turned his eye to the hieroglyphic books inside the cabinet and remembered the day Joan had discovered his gift. He was about seven at the time. Henry remembered gazing at the hieroglyphs above Joan's apothecary door and saying 'know thyself'. Joan had gone crazy because that's what the hieroglyphs had meant, so she had started putting all sorts of foreign languages in front of him and they had discovered that he could close his eyes and understand them. He now tuned in to figure out the title of the book in front of him:

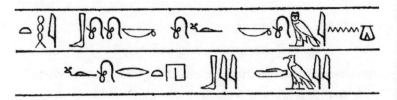

– *The Book of Coming Forth by Day*

Henry placed the books into his bag and was about to walk

away when he noticed an open book on the desk below the cabinet. He noticed a handwritten date and entry and realised it was the duke's diary. Henry could not bring himself to steal the duke's diary – it seemed far too personal. Yet he could not draw his eyes away from it.

Henry flicked through the pages and read a few words of each entry. *The duke was a talented writer*, Henry thought, though he mostly wrote about rich people stuff: horse-riding, fencing, business transactions. Then Henry turned to a page that had an entirely different tone.

Elizabeth and the children took a turn for the worse today. All are bedridden, their sores getting larger by the day. Dr Gilbert says he has done everything he can for them. The rest is up to God. He advised me to leave them in quarantine – as was the proper procedure, apparently – and I almost cut him open. What has proper procedure got to do with a man's family?

Henry flicked again.

Harry passed today. Writing this feels idiotic, vain almost. There are no words. I know countless other parents have lost children to this monster and we all have to die sometime, but there is nothing that can prepare you for the death of a child. It feels as if someone has cut my soul out of my body. Even if the other three survive, things will never be the same, ever.

Then . . .

John died yesterday. There – I wrote it. Died. Not passed, not passed on, not passed away or any of the other pretty nonsense people say to escape the fact of death. Both of my sons are now dead. My wife and my daughter still have the plague and even if Elizabeth recovers I doubt she will ever be strong enough to bear me children again. I shall have no heir. Life is a joke. There is no God; don't believe what these fools tell you. What kind of a God would give you children to love more than you love yourself, only so you could watch them die in agony, screaming and sweating, lying in their own vomit and waste?

Henry could not believe the blasphemy – these words were enough to get you hanged, even if you were a powerful duke. He carried on reading.

Now Catherine too. At least she died peacefully in her sleep, not screaming the house down in pain like the other two. Watching your children die, unable to do anything for them despite living in a palace, despite having everything . . . well, for the first time in my life I think I understand how the peasants must feel – powerless. Truly powerless. I am just waiting for Elizabeth to die now. No point entertaining false hope. My wife will die and I will live on – it's God's cruel joke. Perhaps he knows that I have never believed in him, not even when I was a small boy?

Henry felt strange. He had never known anything about the people whose homes he had robbed before. They were just faceless rich people, social superiors who no doubt would despise Henry whatever he did. But this man with the soldier's face was a loving husband and a caring father, so unlike most of the men Henry knew.

Henry shook himself from his sentimentality and slammed the book shut, realising he'd been reading far longer than he should have. He took the quill and inkpot, stuffed them in his bag with the books and ran out of the study. In the kitchen he found Mary sorting through all the stuff in her sack.

'We've got to go,' Henry told her and Mary sped up her

sorting process.

Henry let out a whistle, hoping Matthew could hear, but there was no response. He whistled again . . . but still nothing.

'Your bloody brother,' Henry said to Mary.

After a pause Mary said, 'Maybe he can't hear you – the walls are pretty thick, you know.'

Henry sighed. 'I suppose we had better go and look for the jolt-head.'

As Henry and Mary turned on to the landing, Henry's stomach nearly emptied itself in shock as the huge wooden front doors swung open.

'Run!' screamed Henry as he spotted Matthew over at the balcony. 'Run, foisters!'

'Get those little rascals,' bellowed the duke, running up the stairs, his bodyguard right behind him. Mary and Henry turned and started sprinting, Mary quickly dropping her bag to gain speed. Henry's spirit sank as he too dropped his, but then he remembered the bird in his pocket. That alone would still make this a very worthwhile score if he got away.

Forget Matthew's prigger, I am keeping that bird, Henry thought. Even though chief priggers were well known for their violence, Henry knew he'd never give up that bird voluntarily now.

The duke and his guard were nearly half-way up the stairs by the time Henry and Mary ran through the kitchen. Henry threw the entire display cabinet of china dishes to the floor behind them, hoping to slow their pursuers down. They sped through a long corridor and seemed to be putting some distance between themselves and the men. Henry had forgotten just how fast Mary was – she could almost keep up with him.

They passed through room after room, slamming doors behind them, throwing over furniture, leaving an incredible trail of carnage as they went. But still the duke and his guard were just a few seconds behind them. One slip and they would be caught for certain. Billy's bloodied and battered face appeared in Henry's mind and propelled his legs faster.

They arrived at a staircase and Henry jumped down five steps at a time, Mary following suit. The men did not have the agility to do the same and Henry smiled as he looked up the staircase – he and Mary were pulling away once more.

They went through another door at the bottom of the stairs and Henry smelled horse manure a split second before he heard the sound of horses. Then he saw them: five beautiful barbary horses, their coats as black as the night sky. He and Mary had ended up in the stables. They had no choice but to run out into the open field to the side of the house, but it would take the duke only seconds to catch them on horseback. Henry thought about stealing one of the horses but saw the locks on the stable fronts. He would never get them free before the duke and his guard got down the stairs.

Stop, thief! Henry saw the face of the man that had sealed Billy's fate with that awful shout; he saw the crowd descend on the little boy, his body disappearing and emerging dead, like the Spanish monkey.

The footsteps pounding down the stairs were getting closer.

Henry could hear the panting of breath.

Not long now.

'Up there,' Mary said, pointing to a stack of hay bales.

She was right. *This* was the only choice.

Henry and Mary climbed up the bales and lay down in the gap between the hay and the ceiling.

Henry heard the opening of the door followed by exhausted breaths and footsteps entering the room. Henry looked over to the other side of the pile of hay, hoping to spot an escape, and a cold, sick feeling ran through him.

A pair of eyes stared back at him. On the floor among the hay was an entire family: mother, father and four children. The mother was awake but the father and children were asleep, oblivious to the commotion occurring around them. The woman had a warm face that reminded Henry of Joan, with freckles and slightly ginger hair, full and curly despite her old age. Her four children all looked to be under ten. One boy and three girls, lying asleep among the hay.

So the duke did have servants, but they lived in the stables with the horses instead of in the servants' quarters. Henry looked into the woman's eyes, petrified, waiting for her to scream and alert the duke to their presence. He thought about all the foisters he'd seen hang, Graham's words ringing in his ears. *You will get caught like all thieves eventually do and you will dance on the rope.*

The duke and his guard barged into the part of the stables where the family slept. 'Oi, wake up, you pock-eaten wretches,' the guard said. The children and father immediately jolted awake. "'Ave you seen them?' the guard barked, as if it was obvious who he was talking about.

Henry held his breath, almost crying in fear. He could hear his heart beating in his ears.

'Seen who?' the lady asked.

Henry was confused. She had definitely seen them.

'Two little thieves. One a Moorish boy and the other a girl,' the duke said, still panting.

'Oh, I thought I heard something outside in the field,' the woman said.

Henry could not believe she was lying for them. The relief that washed over him was as intense as the fear that it replaced.

'Why didn't you wake me?' the woman's husband demanded, both his tone of voice and his look carrying threats.

'Don't just lie there, help us find them,' the duke commanded.

'Yes, woman, help,' the servant's husband barked.

The duke and his guard ran out towards the front of the stables, the entire family following fast. The woman did not look back up at Henry and he wished he could thank her for lying for them. He had no idea why she would take a risk like that for a total stranger.

'What shall we do?' Mary whispered.

Henry tried to think, but his mind was paralysed by fear. He'd never come this close to being caught. All he could think about were the warnings Graham had given him and how he wished he'd listened. All he could see were the faces of dead thieves and how he'd sworn that would never be him. Yet here he was, on the verge of getting caught by a duke so pernicious that he had his servants sleep in the barn. *What would such a man do to thieves?*

'We can't stay here,' Henry said. 'It'll only be a matter of time before they find us. Let's go back upstairs. If we get to the kitchen we can jump from that window down to the field by the lake. That makes more sense than running out of the front door into that big open space.'

'Ay,' Mary said.

Henry took a deep breath, muttered a few good-luck words to himself and started to climb down the bales of hay backwards. Mary followed, and they crept back towards the staircase. Henry opened the door slowly, silently. They tiptoed through the door and closed it quietly behind them. Henry's heart started to regain something like a regular beat.

'There they are!' a child's voice shouted.

Henry and Mary didn't wait to see if the duke or his guard had heard; they just sprinted up the stairs towards the kitchen. Henry's lungs were burning in his chest by the time he'd reached the top of the staircase, but he could not stop. They ran back through the rooms they had trashed, hopping over furniture and smashed cabinets.

Finally, they arrived in the kitchen. Henry got to the window first and smashed it with the back of his fist, scraping away as much glass as he had time for.

'You go first,' he said to Mary.

'But—'

'We don't have time for arguments,' Henry cut in.

Mary stepped up on to the window ledge and crawled through the gap.

'Jump!' Henry shouted.

Mary looked back at him.

'Jump!' Henry screamed. He could hear the thudding of footsteps in the next room. The men would be through the kitchen door any second. As Henry got up on to the window ledge and started to crawl out, he heard the kitchen doors slam open and panicked, scraping his back nastily on the jagged glass. He let out a muted yelp, even though it was too late to worry about alerting his pursuers, and then felt a hand grab his trailing ankle.

Henry turned to see the duke's guard, face twisted in anger, his hand gripping Henry's foot.

Henry kicked out at the guard's face – hard enough to loosen his grip – and scrambled through the window on to the small ledge beside Mary. He took her hand.

'Let's jump together,' Henry said, and Mary nodded. The first-storey window was not so high that jumping from it would kill anybody, but it was certainly high enough that it could mean a broken leg.

Henry squeezed Mary's hand and jumped. In that moment, Henry felt Mary's grip loosen and then let go. It happened in a split second – Mary's hand was yanked from his by the speed of his falling. He landed with a thud that sent a jolting pain through his whole body and looked back up at the window.

Mary was dangling upside down, her ankle in the grip of the duke's bodyguard, only having managed to avoid smashing her face on the side of the building because her shoulder had got there first.

Henry stared at the duke's guard and he stared back at Henry. The guard had the same face that tough men have had for all eternity. His skin was rough as sand with lines that were not wrinkles nor scars but tough-guy marks, as if the battles he had seen had traced a map on to his face. He had a beard that was neither clean-shaven nor scruffily overgrown, but just enough to exude aggression. He had solid, angular cheekbones and a jawline that would have made another man handsome, but just made him look as if he ran through walls head-first.

As the man stared into Henry's face with his bloodshot eyes, Henry knew that running was useless. This man was not someone who forgot a face, especially one as easily identifiable as Henry's. Besides, he could hardly leave Mary with a monster like that.

'Come back into the house, knave,' the man shouted, 'or I'll drop this little wench on 'er face.'

Henry knew that he meant it.

They live for a time in the kingdom founded by
Sunjata – who some call usurper – and there the
general and his daughter learn the art of writing.
But again war comes and again they flee.
Ogun, God of iron and war, is eating well.

9

Henry fought the urge to scream, the veins in his neck burning under the strain. Another lash, another wince, and then another and another as the nine-clawed whip lashed Henry's bare back. The nine-clawed whip, the scourge of every pauper in Britain – nine thin strands of knotted cord that tore at the skin like an animal's teeth.

Despite the pain, Mary and Matthew dominated his thoughts; he prayed they were not beating Mary like this and he hoped Matthew had actually got away.

The whip lashed into the gash that Henry had got from climbing through the window and he just could not contain the pain any more.

'Arrrghhh! You flea-bitten son-of-a-doxy,' Henry shouted, tears of rage shooting from his eyes. He pulled against the metal chains that held his hands to the wall and the duke's guard started to laugh. He paused with the whipping but Henry kept raging. 'You fishmonger, you sister-fiddler, you dirty knave! You'd better not be doing this to Mary!' Henry immediately hated himself for revealing her name.

Tell them nothing or tell them lies, Moll Cutpurse had always told him.

'More,' the duke commanded and his guard began lashing

Henry's blood-soaked back again, each whip feeling like it was cutting Henry's body in half.

Henry's mind flashed with the similar beatings he had got from Agnes: the time she had broken his fingers with a metal rod when he was seven; the time she'd beaten him with a broken tree branch so badly that he had almost passed out; the times she had made all three of the children queue up to be whipped on their legs with a spiky wire – Henry still had the scars where she'd torn his flesh. She always made sure Henry got the worst of it.

Henry did not have the strength to rage any more, but started to sob and whimper. As each blow landed, his cries grew more and more pathetic, until he collapsed into a pile on the floor with his arms painfully stretched upwards, still chained to the wall.

'Please stop,' Henry begged. 'Please, please stop.' Out of the corner of his eye Henry saw the duke raise his hand and finally the beating ceased.

The duke came close to Henry, inserted his fingers into Henry's thick, curly hair and yanked Henry's head up towards him.

'This is what happens when you steal from me. You broke my china, you tore my paintings, you smashed up my beautiful home and you dared to kick my guard in the face, you reckless little Moor. I am not done with you, not by a long way.' The duke walked off, slammed the cell door shut and left Henry bloody and crying in the dark.

Henry could not tell if he had been cuffed to the wall for hours or days. He had blacked out a few times but remembered someone bringing him water and some dry bread. He thought it was the same servant woman who had lied for him in the barn, but he was so disorientated that he could not be certain.

What do they have planned for me? he wondered, telling himself that his fear was gone, that he would accept the rest of his fate stoically once he knew what it was. *More beatings? The stocks? Hard labour? If they were planning to kill me or hand me over to the authorities to be hanged they would have already done so*, he reasoned – or at least he hoped.

The duke came down the stairs again, walking slowly. Henry wondered what kind of a man had a dungeon in his own home. *The kind of man who has his own servants sleep in the barn, that's who.*

Behind the duke followed his guard, carrying a flaming torch. Henry fought to suppress a flinch as he imagined more beatings. The guard also carried the sack Henry had left behind at the scene of the crime. Henry felt the golden bird scratch at the inside of his leg and knew the most sensible thing to do would be to give that up too.

The duke pulled up a chair and sat staring intently through the bars of the cell at Henry. He gestured to the sack and his guard dumped it on the ground. The duke looked at Henry, not with accusation or even anger, but what seemed like confusion.

The duke started to empty the contents of the sack. 'One silver plate – cost, ten shillings.' He placed it on the floor.

125

'Two gold rings – cost, ten pounds. Sweetmeat bowl carved in Benin – ten shillings. I can imagine that one might be of sentimental value to you.'

Benin? Was the duke alluding to his mother? *No, it's just a coincidence, Henry. Stop being silly.*

'So, all of this makes sense to me,' the duke said, after he'd placed all the items down neatly. 'The usual stuff a common thief would pilfer. I'd be happy to have your hands off and give you back to those bloody witches, but first I must satisfy my own curiosity.'

How does the duke know about Agnes and Joan? Henry wondered. *Has he made Mary talk?* Henry dreaded to think what they had done to her.

The duke took the books out of the bag and read out each title as he went. '*The Epic of Gilgamesh*, *The Republic*, *Book of the Marvels of the World*, *Alexander's Journey Up Country from the Sea*.' The duke paused and looked to Henry again with confusion behind his angry brow.

He looked down and stared at the books. 'Who asked you to steal these particular books from me?' Henry didn't know what to say. 'These books are not randomly selected, little boy. Their choice alone reflects a great knowledge. Who asked you to get these from me? Which man of quality?'

'No one did,' said Henry.

'Listen, little boy, if you don't tell me now, my friend here has plenty more of what he gave you earlier.'

'Nobody asked me – I chose them,' Henry repeated, trying his best not to sound defiant. He really did not want another beating.

The duke laughed mockingly. 'So, I suppose you can read the finer points of Plato then?' He nodded to his guard, who unlocked Henry's cell and unchained Henry's hands from the wall. The duke followed him into the cell and tossed the copy of Plato's *Republic* at Henry. 'Go on then, read,' the duke said to Henry and looked at his guard, tapping him to share in the joke. 'The little knave is going to give us a story.' The guard pointed his flaming torch towards Henry so he could see the pages. Henry savoured the light and the warmth.

He was so weak he could barely pick up the book, his hands shaking as if it were a heavy weight. But he managed to open the first page and read, '*I went down yesterday to the Piraeus with Glaucon, the son of Ariston, to pay my devotions to the Goddess . . .*' Henry struggled to get the words out, but it was clear that he could read.

'Stop, wait . . . what?' The duke could not utter a coherent sentence.

Henry stopped reading and looked up. Even in his pain he relished the look of shock on the duke's face. He'd underestimated Henry, and Henry had proven him wrong.

The duke grabbed the book from Henry and flipped to a random page. 'Read this one instead,' he barked.

'*Hope, he says, cherishes the soul of him who lives in justice and holiness,*' Henry read, delighting in the duke's distress and unable to resist the temptation to show off.

'Wait a minute, how about this one?' the duke said in a tone that seemed as if he did not really want an answer to his question. This time he handed the book to Henry delicately, as if it were a prized possession. It was the one with the hieroglyphs. 'Can y-you read th-this one?' the duke stuttered.

'Yeah, but it's different when it's not English or Greek or Latin. Pass me a quill and paper please.'

The duke gestured to his guard, who ripped a blank page from the end of one of the books. He passed it to Henry, along with the quill and inkpot that he had taken from the bag. Henry put his hand over the book and closed his eyes, waiting for the shapes and colours and sounds to appear to him. As they translated themselves into English, he scribbled them down on the paper.

She was the primeval ocean and she emerged as herself of herself and all has come forth through and from her. She is self-existent, and her nature is secret, a mystery to all.

'So it's true,' the duke muttered. Henry thought that was a strange thing to say. 'Who taught you to do this' – the duke broke off, clearly searching for the correct word to describe what he had just seen – 'magic?'

The duke had said 'magic' in such a disgusted way that Henry thought he had made a mistake. His ego had got the better of him. Why had he needed to show the duke his gift? Why had he not stopped to think about it for just one second?

He could have just left it at reading Latin and Greek. Even reading English was a strange enough thing for a poor child without any formal schooling. But instead he had shown the duke more of his gift, just to show off. *What an idiot*, he thought, bracing himself for the duke's reaction. Magic – like anything powerful people did not understand, or could not control – was heavily frowned upon.

But the look in the duke's eye seemed resentful and capricious and, yet, full of admiration. It was both scary and satisfying, because it reminded Henry so much of the way he himself looked at rich people.

'I don't think it's magic, sir, and nobody taught me,' Henry said.

'You put your hand over a book and translate it with your eyes closed and you don't think that is magic?' The duke laughed.

'When you put it like that.' Henry let out a crack of a smile.

'The innocence of youth, I suppose. You have no idea how valuable this magic is. I have no doubt those crafty old hags have done their best to keep you ignorant of that all these years.'

Again Henry wondered how the duke knew about Joan and Agnes. Thoughts of Mary and Matthew came into his head once more.

The duke looked to his bodyguard and back, commanding, 'Fetch Camilla.'

The guard left the room, returning moments later with the woman that Henry had locked eyes with in the barn. *So that's her name*, Henry thought, *Camilla*.

She came into Henry's cell carrying a tray with ointments and wraps and placed the tray on the ground next to him. 'This will sting a little,' she said, handing him a rag. 'Take this to bite on.'

Camilla definitely reminded Henry of Joan, even though they did not look alike. There was a pain and kindness in her eyes that was unmistakably similar, but Camilla seemed much more subservient than he could ever imagine Joan being. Every second or two, she looked round at the duke and his guard as if to get their approval for each movement.

Camilla applied the ointment to Henry's back and he felt a burn that was almost equal to being whipped. He shoved the rag in his mouth and bit down on it to mute his screams. The duke and his guard stayed watching over Henry and Camilla the whole time, so he could not talk to her, but her looks and her gentle touch let him know she was a friend – if lying for him had not made that clear already.

Why would a woman who is so clearly scared risk herself for me? Henry kept asking himself as he grunted and groaned his way through having his wounds cleaned. *Why is this evil duke letting me get cleaned up? What is he planning?*

Eventually, Camilla finished and Henry was left with a numb, hot ache all over his back. She lit a few candles around Henry's cell, then packed up her things and walked out, the guard re-locking the cell.

'Where's my friend?' Henry finally asked.

'Translate that book I gave you, Henry,' the duke said, his guard tossing Henry a notebook of blank paper. They left Henry alone once again with just his thoughts and the books.

On camel they cross unending desert.

With the stars as their path they pray to Oludumare,

the supreme creator to guide them.

They pray to Olokun, God of the oceans.

And by boat the general and his daughter sail on the

mighty sea to the land of the strangers.

Henry was not good with boredom. Pain, grief and anger he could do. Henry was used to these and had found strategies for coping with them. But boredom drove him to his wits' end.

It had only taken him an hour to translate the hieroglyphic book and now Henry was staring at the spare blank pages of the notebook. He had the urge to write, but he thought better of it, not knowing how the duke would react to him using the paper for his own musings. Paper was not cheap, after all. Henry tapped the quill on his thigh and brushed his barely existing moustache with his fingers, the boredom almost threatening to burst out of him. He managed to get up and stumble around the cell, looking for something to do despite his pain.

Henry noticed that the walls were caked in a layer of green slime and mud. He looked at the quill, then back at the walls and had an idea. He held the quill to the wall and scraped. The slime came away in a neat line, leaving a clear mark on the wall. *This wall will be my paper*. Henry smiled. He thought about his last week, about his mother, about always feeling like a foreigner in the only land he had ever known. His hand started to carve words into the wall's dirt.

Origin unknown.

Henry gazed at the letters, really thinking about the magic of writing. *A person could come here one hundred years from now and read my words*, he thought. Writing on the wall was greater, more permanent, more important than writing on paper. He felt like one of the scribes he had read about in the ancient lands of Egypt and Mesopotamia who had supposedly carved entire books on to the walls of stone temples. He wondered if the book he had just translated had originally been carved into some stone temple?

Henry looked down at his brown skin, his badge of difference, and his thoughts returned to his own origins. He completed the other half of the opening line.

My colour, my clue.

He thought about the ships on the Thames, wondering where his mother had come from and what had brought her to these shores. Another line came to him.

Past seas and sands, the land of my mother

He thought about the baker's son and the child at the well and the way the duke had called him 'Moor' as if he were a thing, not a person.

The place that I know sees only in hue
I am what I am – man, but not brother

Henry had never thought much about his father, perhaps because it was his mother's blackness that had defined so much of his life. Another couplet came to him.

Father departed, as often the way
I am what I am; the bastard I be

Henry thought about the other slum children he knew. Many of them had absent fathers, but almost all knew their mothers. Even doxies care for their children, Henry thought.

Yet even night women often display
Such care, attention, I never did see

Words flowed out of Henry now, and he kept scrawling on the wall.

What curse is my flesh? The heavens doth tell
The womb of time so did freeze at my birth
I am what I am, no story to sell
No mother have I. So what am I worth?

Henry read back the sonnet so far. It seemed depressing, almost self-pitying. Despite everything Henry had been through, he knew he was clever and strong. Despite the way people treated him, he had always felt that he was special somehow. He wasn't afraid to admit these things. The final two lines came to him.

Yet skill and quick wit doth follow my name
With wit and quick skill, the bastard slew shame

Henry read the whole sonnet out loud, as if he were acting on a stage, walking around the cell and performing to himself with grand hand gestures.

> *Origin unknown. My colour, my clue.*
> *Past seas and sands, the land of my mother*
> *The place that I know sees only in hue*
> *I am what I am – man, but not brother*
> *Father departed, as often the way*
> *I am what I am; the bastard I be*
> *Yet even night women often display*
> *Such care, attention, I never did see*
> *What curse is my flesh? The heavens doth tell*
> *The womb of time so did freeze at my birth*
> *I am what I am, no story to sell*
> *No mother have I. So what am I worth?*
> *Yet skill and quick wit doth follow my name*
> *With wit and quick skill, the bastard slew shame*

Henry wrote and wrote, powered by a feverish energy. He even forgot the pain of his wounds. He carved sonnet after sonnet into his cell wall, all arranged in a neat grid to preserve space and numbered in order so he would be able to read back the sequence of his thoughts.

Time passed and Henry's energy faded as hunger and anger at his situation took over again. But he fought to keep his negative feelings at bay and looked back over his work – thirteen sonnets in all, and he was very pleased with them.

There was a sonnet about stealing that he thought particularly witty, and he performed it to himself.

I take what I see but thief I am not
The world took from me before I could mourn
What thief could I be? When the stars did plot
To steal my parents before I was born
Dump me with witches, evil as Agnes
Beatings and hunger and insult I bear
However you name; it's more than sadness
For me no gods nor god ever did care
So property I borrow, keep and sell
I know I could hang for deeds that I do
Life is for living not thinking of hell
So take, I take a shilling. Or a few
The stars doth smile down on me in one way
I have not hung, yet I steal every day

Henry heard footsteps coming down the stairs. He scrambled to move the candles he had assembled in his writing corner and spread them back around the cell so that the duke would not see his sonnets. He sighed deeply with relief when Camilla came into the dungeon, but to his chagrin she was quickly followed by the duke's guard.

'Time for grub,' Camilla said and the guard opened Henry's cell.

Camilla placed a tray with bread and water down in front of Henry. 'Let me get a look at those cuts please.' She said it as if Henry were a child who had fallen over and banged his knee.

Henry took off his top and turned round so Camilla could see his back properly.

'I'm sorry, but this will hurt again,' Camilla said. 'Though not as much as last time.'

As Camilla washed Henry's back and Henry forced muffled groans into a rag, the duke's guard sniggered at his pain. Henry remembered that he had kicked the guard in the face and that made him smile inside.

Henry noticed Camilla keep looking behind her at the duke's guard with the same expression of fear and approval-seeking that she had with the duke.

As she worked, Camilla dropped a small cloth on to Henry's top – he assumed so the guard could not see it. The cloth unwrapped itself a little as it landed and Henry could make out a scone and what looked like some sort of meat. He fought the urge to hug Camilla or say thank you and instead simply turned and smiled at her.

Camilla smiled back.

Why does this woman keep risking herself for me? What does she want? Henry's thoughts ran in circles as he tried not to stare at the scone, his stomach churning in anticipation.

Camilla finished and packed up her things. As she walked back out of the cell, Henry folded up his shirt to cover the extra food.

'Please let the duke know I have finished this book,' Henry said and he handed Camilla the notebook and the original text through the bars.

Perhaps an hour later, the duke's guard returned with a box full of books and enough paper and ink for Henry to translate the whole lot.

'Courtesy of My Lord Wilmslow,' the guard said.

'Where's my friend?' Henry tried to sound demanding but the duke's guard just laughed and walked back out of the cell.

Henry kicked the box of books, cracking its side. He grunted and walked around his cell mumbling profanities for a while, before slumping back to the floor.

He looked over to his folded shirt. He'd been saving the food Camilla had brought, but couldn't wait any longer. He unwrapped his shirt and quickly devoured the scone. It was stale and tough but the butter and jam in its middle was fresh. It tasted heavenly. There were also two pieces of meat and one boiled potato, but he'd wait to eat those. He had no idea when he would next be getting some food. *Whatever her motives, God bless Camilla.*

Henry spent the next few days translating and writing sonnets and tried to think about Mary as little as possible. In between bread and water meals – and the extra bits Camilla managed to sneak him – he tried to exercise in the cell and keep his limbs warm. After much begging, the duke agreed to let Camilla bring him hot water and towels to wash himself with every other day. The washing and the food made the cell bearable, but there was no escaping how lonely and bored he was – even with all the books in the world.

He thought about Joan and he wondered again what had happened to Matthew. He presumed he had got away as otherwise Matthew would surely be in the dungeon too, but there was no way to know for sure – this duke might have many more places to keep his prisoners. He thought about the Gap and his friends, the football games and the thrill of catching a coney. He prayed to God for some kind of magic that could lift him out of this cell and take him back to his home.

Henry spotted the duke quietly spying on him a few times through the main gate to the dungeon. He did not know what to make of it. The duke did not walk off in shame once Henry had noticed him, he did not smile nor grimace; he simply sat there staring until Henry continued with his work and then eventually he would vanish.

What will become of me? Henry couldn't help thinking. Somehow he felt that his mother would protect him.

But it is said the general is cursed.

11

Henry was deep in the flow of translating when he sensed a presence that made him uneasy. He broke from the state and opened his eyes.

He was startled to the see the duke, his guard and two other men standing outside his cell. One of the men was wearing a doctor's uniform, with a double eyepatch and a large mask in the shape of a bird's beak, along with the gloves and gown that made doctors look a lot like executioners. The other unknown man wore exquisitely expensive clothes and shoes, but had a large crystal hanging around his neck and a long flowing beard. This contrast made him look like a cross between a nobleman and a wizard. The presence of these two new men gave Henry the sudden feeling that he was on trial.

'Open,' the duke commanded. His guard opened Henry's cell, but the duke and the men did not yet enter.

'Stand up,' the duke barked at Henry, and though Henry was still irritated at being barked at he noted something new in the Duke's voice. Instead of his usual self-assured, patronising tone it seemed like the Duke was showing off. As Henry stood up he tried to guess which of these men the duke wanted to impress so badly.

The three men entered his cell and Henry did not bow,

feeling a small sense of victory in this little act of defiance.

'This is Dr Dee.' The duke gestured to the man with the crystal and then to the man with the bird mask. 'And this is Dr Gilbert.'

Henry tried not to stare at the eyes dancing around behind the two small holes in the mask, though he pictured the face behind it. He imagined it to be repulsive, wrinkled and probably pock-marked.

Dr Dee cleared his throat and started to speak. His voice had a smooth, knowing authority behind it that reminded Henry of Graham. 'Henry, I have heard very much about your magic from old Wilmslow here.'

Henry had to fight back the urge to snigger at the way Dr Dee addressed the duke – *old Wilmslow*, not Lord Wilmslow, not Sir Wilmslow, but 'old'.

'But I must confess, even though I have known Charles since we were children' – Henry noticed the duke shuffle uncomfortably, clearly annoyed at being referred to so informally – 'I thought what I was being told was wholly fantastical. I have been studying magic for a lifetime and I have never even read about a gift such as yours, much less seen it in action.' Dr Dee stroked his long beard in slow, measured movements as he spoke, making him seem ever more wizardly. 'Myself and Dr Gilbert here will need to run some tests on you for the purpose of trying to understand your magic. Some of them may well be painful, but pain is a necessary component in the pursuit of knowledge. You of all people must surely understand that?'

'Do I have a choice?' Henry asked.

'Of course not, you insolent wretch,' the duke said, scowling.

Dr Dee smiled so politely that he may as well have laughed in Henry's face. 'You are a bright lad, Henry. If I were in your position' – Dr Dee paused to look around the cell as if to point out just how disgusting Henry's surroundings were – 'I would make it a priority to understand that one has to have leverage before one can negotiate.' Henry held the doctor's gaze. 'However, I believe I'll also give you good reason to co-operate with us.' There was a sudden chirp to Dr Dee's tone. 'As I for one cannot work down here in this dark, damp flea-pit. If you promise to be on your best behaviour I am sure Charles will let you up into the house so we can work on you there.'

Henry tried not to let his excitement about getting out of the dungeon show on his face but inside he was dreaming of finding Mary and of running away back home.

Dr Dee looked to the duke, his eyes pressuring Wilmslow to agree. The duke swallowed his scowl and forced a clearly pained smile on to his face.

'Well, *John*.' The duke said Dr Dee's first name with a pettiness and Henry saw Dr Dee smile as if he too had noticed it. 'It would have been nice if we'd discussed that as an option. Henry is my prisoner, after all, and let's not allow his . . . *talents* –' the duke uttered the word as if it was a painful admission – 'to let us forget why he is—'

Dr Dee cut in. 'I totally understand your plight, Charles, and I am sorry for not checking with you before, but it just came to me as I was standing here.' Dr Dee bowed to the duke.

'I'm sorry, Charles, but I would have to concur,' said Dr Gilbert through his mask, his voice high-pitched and surprisingly young-sounding. 'The fetid smell could unbalance a man's humours and lead to illness. I'm not sure it's wise to keep a prisoner of such extraordinary value down here.'

A prisoner of such extraordinary value, Henry repeated to himself.

'Well, gentlemen, it's easy to forgive a crime of which one is not the victim.' The duke managed to suppress his irritation with dignity. 'I am sure if it were your home thus violated you may feel differently, but nonetheless I shall agree, on one condition. Henry must wear wrist irons. I don't want his light fingers getting any ideas.' The duke glared at Henry, warning written in his eyes, and Henry tried to suppress the flashbacks of being tied to the wall and beaten.

'Agreed,' Dr Gilbert said.

'John?'

'Agreed,' Dr Dee said, though Henry could tell that he wanted to object.

Dr Dee turned to Henry. 'So, Henry, are you going to make me regret asking my friend to let you out of here?'

'No sir, I'll be on my best behaviour, I promise,' Henry said, knowing full well that he would run away at the first opportunity.

Henry came up from the dungeon flanked by the duke's guard,

the two doctors and the duke himself. His rusty wrist irons scraped against his skin and rattled as he walked. His eyes stung and watered as he struggled to adjust to his first glimpse of natural light in what must have been at least a couple of weeks. Once his eyes had settled, he took in the duke's house, which seemed even more beautiful than before, with every inch of the staircase decorated with elaborate paintings of forests and rivers, battles and pageants.

As they passed the kitchen, Henry saw Camilla and her daughters preparing food. He smiled and Camilla smiled back pleasantly, but Henry could sense something else in her eyes – shock or fear, he could not tell.

'Henry!' a voice screamed.

Henry turned to see Mary at the other side of the kitchen, running towards him. He felt warm at the sight of her, but her eyes disturbed him even more than Camilla's had.

'Mary, get back to work,' Camilla shouted.

The duke's guard stood forward to block Mary as she drew near.

'What have you done to him?' Mary said, staring at Henry as if she could not believe what she was seeing. It was only then that Henry looked down at himself and noticed how much weight he had lost, how his body was covered in flea bites and how dirt and gunk stuck to his skin and hair, despite his best attempts to wash it off. He knew that his punishment could have been far worse, but Henry still despised the duke and his guard for doing this to him.

'Get back to the kitchen, you low-born tallow-hatch,' the duke bellowed. His guard picked Mary up and started to carry her back, leaving Henry unattended.

Henry pictured himself making a run for it – running back to Joan, to the Gap and to all that was familiar – but the weight of his irons told him it would be futile, for now at least.

As the guard put Mary down, Camilla held her by the arms and spoke sternly. 'By George, don't be such an ungrateful brat, Mary.'

'Look at him! He looks like a half-dead starving beggar, you jackdaw!' Mary shouted across the room at the duke.

Camilla slapped Mary across the face with such force that it nearly knocked her over. Henry wanted to scream out, to go and help Mary, the way she had just tried to help him, but he only stood there and wondered how sweet, scared Camilla could be the same woman who slapped Mary like that.

Dr Dee whispered in the duke's ear, whose face turned sour.

'Camilla, take Mary to fix Henry a bath and make sure it is she who cleans it up afterwards,' the duke commanded. 'Also have her prepare him some food, with no help from you. If she wants to make sure the Moor is clean she can do so, in addition to all her other chores.'

'Yes, sir,' Camilla said and nudged Mary.

'Ay,' Mary said without looking up.

Camilla nudged her again.

'I mean, yes, sir,' Mary said with a curtsy.

'And, Mary,' Dr Dee said calmly, 'take a leaf out of this

woman's book and learn some gratitude. You and Henry should have danced on the rope for what you did. But thanks to our gracious duke here, you are alive and living in a palace that the likes of you would never have a hope of even setting foot in ordinarily.'

The likes of you, Henry repeated in his head. Despite his pretend kindness, what Dr Dee *really* thought of poor people was now obvious.

Camilla nudged Mary again.

'Yes, sir,' Mary said.

As Henry took off his breeches he felt the golden bird scratch his thigh. He took the bird out of the secret pocket and removed it from its pouch. The impact of its beauty was as powerful as the first time he had seen it. He was reminded of his evolving sonnet.

The Bird, the Ship, what's freedom and meaning
Our ships move only with wind or labour

He played around a little in his mind until a rhyming couplet to match came to him:

The bird does not try, flying is breathing
The cost of ship is death to the sailor

Henry smiled, noticed the pile of clothes on the floor and then panicked. He could not conceal the bird on his body if his breeches were taken away; he urgently needed a new hiding place for it. Henry returned the bird to its pouch and looked around the room, taking in the whitewashed wooden-panelled walls and bare wooden floor. There was a sink made from some sort of precious stone and a large wooden bathtub full to the brim with water. It let off a thin layer of steam, the smells of lavender and rose filling the air.

'Where can I hide you?' Henry spoke out loud as if addressing the bird. He got on his hands and knees and started to push floorboards, hoping one of them would be loose enough that he could slip the bird underneath. He crawled around the room, pushing board after board, to no avail.

Henry got back on his feet. The bathtub rested on four gold legs shaped like an animal's paws. He returned to his hands and knees and put his head half-way under the bath to examine the legs. They had a kind of hollow back part. If only Henry could lift the bathtub, he might be able to slip the bird underneath one of the feet.

Henry placed the bird on the floor right next to one of the legs and stood up.

He grabbed the bath by the rim and gave a stiff pull to feel its weight. It really was heavy. He looked down at the bird. *But I only have to move it an inch*, he said to himself. Henry steadied his breath and pulled at the bath again. It did not budge.

Henry paused for breath, grimaced, and this time pulled

with as much force as he could. Slowly, the bath came up from the floor, just slightly. Already Henry's wrists and arms were burning but he pulled even harder and it shifted a little more. He pulled again, his back and thighs shaking and his breath heavy now. Henry quickly nudged the bird into place with his toe before he collapsed and dropped the bath.

The pouch disappeared under its foot. Henry felt like he'd miss the bird somehow, but at least it was well hidden.

Henry put his toe in the bath-water and then his whole foot. It was a little too hot but he held it there for a few moments to get used to the warmth. He put the other foot in, waited a minute, then climbed into the tub and lay down, letting the water massage his body. The warmth worked its way into his joints and eased all the stiffness and pain. He washed his hair, face and body with imported Castille soap – made from olive oil rather than the cheap animal-fat soap he was used to. How strange it was that the English hated the Spaniards, yet so much great stuff seemed to come from there.

It was the first time in his life that he had been fully submerged in warm water. He dreamed of being rich and owning his own tub.

Memories of cold winter washes out by the well flooded in: the way the near-frozen water made him cold through to his bones, Joan washing him when he was just a little boy. He wished Joan could have a bath and he swore to himself that if ever he had enough money, he would buy her one. He wondered if Matthew had made it back home to tell Joan what had happened.

A knock sounded at the door. 'Hurry up, Moor,' the duke's guard said.

Henry wanted to groan in protest. He closed his eyes and tried to capture the feeling of warmth before he got out, dried himself and started to dress.

The thick woollen nethersocks pulled all the way up past his knee and gave his legs a feeling of comfort they had never known. The breeches were similarly thick, black and without a single stain. The shirt was a smooth, fine linen of the type Henry had only stolen before but could never afford to keep, and the ruff was made of a similar fabric. Henry spent several minutes just feeling and staring at it until another knock at the door hurried him along.

Hung on the back of the door was a thick black cloak. Henry did not know what to do with it – only men of importance wore cloaks and it was illegal for commoners to do so. *Did the duke leave this here as a test, or a joke?* he asked himself.

'Excuse me, sir!' Henry shouted through the door.

'What?' the duke's guard replied.

'Do I wear this caster, sir?'

'Just get dressed, boy. Put on whatever has been left for you to wear, and do it quickly.' The resentment in the guard's voice suggested Henry was indeed supposed to wear the cloak.

'Yes, sir,' Henry replied, pulling the cloak on and stroking it for a minute. Then he spotted the shoes. Henry picked them up and sniffed them. They had certainly been worn a lot and the leather was starting to turn smelly, but nonetheless . . . *They are*

Spanish leather. Henry could not believe it. Never in his life did he think he'd get to wear a pair of Spanish leather shoes, not even a duke's old cast-offs.

He slipped the shoes on and walked out of the washing place almost feeling like a rich man. But as the duke's guard put the wrist irons back on, Henry remembered what he actually was – *a prisoner of extraordinary value*.

The guard led Henry to the dining hall where Camilla served Henry a large bowl of porridge that he managed to eat furiously, even with the wrist irons on. As his full stomach weighed him down pleasantly, clothed in a noble's cloak, his body still feeling fresh and warm from the bath, Henry battled with himself. He knew they were trying to buy his obedience, to placate him with comfort and trinkets but he could not deny that he felt a thousand times better than he had an hour ago.

The duke's guard led Henry up the stairs and into a room that the doctors had converted into something like an experimentation chamber. There were tools and contraptions laid out on a desk to one side, where Dr Gilbert was standing, and a shelf full of glass jars containing brightly coloured potions, animal tongues and snake skins on the other. It all reminded Henry of the line from *Romeo and Juliet* about apothecaries:

> *A tortoise hung,*
> *An alligator stuffed, and other skins*
> *Of ill shaped fishes*

Dr Dee gestured to the duke's guard to unshackle Henry and leave the room. Once the guard closed the door behind him, Dr Dee finally spoke.

'Now, Henry, before we begin, I just need to ask you a few questions about this magic of yours.'

Henry was still assessing the room. There was a thick cloth covering the floors, as if the doctors were expecting them to be stained. He tried to stop himself imagining what tortures might await him. He also noticed that Dr Gilbert still wore his mask and gloves, even though they were no longer in the dungeon. Did he believe that Henry was sick, or cursed, or something?

Dr Dee gestured for Henry to sit down in a chair in the middle of the room. Dr Gilbert tied Henry's arms to the chair with thick leather straps and walked back to the desk where Henry could no longer see him, because the chair he was strapped to faced the other wall.

'When were you born, and where?' Dr Dee asked.

'I dunno when, but right here in London,' Henry replied.

'What do you mean you don't know when?'

'The likes of us don't get our birth dates recorded you know. I'm from the Gap.'

Henry said *the Gap* with both pride and shame. Young men raised in the Gap had a well-earned reputation for toughness, but it came with an equal reputation for poverty and filth.

'I see,' Dr Dee said as he walked behind the chair as if to hand the conversation to Dr Gilbert. Now Henry could not see either of them but he could hear a grinding or sharpening of metal – perhaps the tools that had been on the desk. He tried his best not to feel unsettled.

'Do you pray regularly, Henry?' Dr Gilbert barked.

'Yes, every day, sir,' Henry lied. He only prayed when he really wanted something from God.

'Church?' Dr Gilbert demanded.

'Every Sunday, like everyone else.'

'Do you recognise Jesus Christ as our one true lord and saviour?'

'Yes, of course,' Henry replied.

'Yet you are a thief who cavorts with witches?' Dr Gilbert shrieked.

'Gilbert,' Dr Dee interrupted. 'I entreat thee, please, to focus on trying to understand Henry's gift rather than preaching a sermon.' Dr Dee walked back in front of Henry. 'Lord Wilmslow tells us that nobody taught you this gift. Is that true?'

Still Henry could hear the metal tools grinding behind his head, the sharp sounds breaking his concentration.

'Ay.'

'Are you sure of that?'

'Yes, sir.'

'So how did you know you could do it?'

Before Henry could answer, Dr Gilbert walked round in front of him and stood behind Dr Dee. He was holding one of the sharpened tools up to the window light, examining it. Henry took in the curved silver blade, the shape of a half moon, with a point as fine as a pinprick and a surface fit for shaving silk. It looked as if it were designed to tear out a man's guts in one move.

Henry could not tell if Dr Gilbert's mask was meant to be deliberately intimidating, but he imagined a wicked grin on the pock-marked face under that mask; a man just waiting to cut him open and hear him scream.

'Henry?' Dr Dee urged.

Henry did not like feeling intimidated. He'd seen far worse than some posh doctors sharpening a blade and he'd be damned if he'd let these fools bully him into telling them his life story.

'I dunno,' Henry replied, thinking back to the day Joan had first discovered his gift.

'I don't remember when I first realised I could do it,' Henry lied, feeling power in his ability to keep back what information he wanted.

'That's because it's witchcraft!' Dr Gilbert cried, waving his blade wildly. 'Witchcraft, I tell you!'

'Easy, Gilbert,' Dr Dee told him. 'Henry, I want you to describe exactly what happens when you are translating.'

'It's hard to explain,' Henry replied.

'Well, we are going to need you to try. We don't want to run the wrong tests on you now, do we?'

'That could put you in very serious danger,' Dr Gilbert chimed in, pointing his blade at Henry like a master's finger.

Screw this lot and their danger, Henry thought.

'I can't describe it. I just close my eyes and it happens.'

Dr Gilbert walked back to his desk and Henry heard him scribble some notes. He reappeared in front of Henry, holding a cup in one hand, his blade still in the other.

'Drink it.'

Henry looked to Dr Dee, who nodded at him to comply.

'Best to down it in one go – it will help with the pain,' Dr Dee said.

'What is it?' Henry asked.

'I can't describe it,' Dr Gilbert replied and Henry found it amusing that a grown man was being so petty. Dr Gilbert raised the cup, Henry opened his mouth and felt the liquid pour in. It stank and it tasted revolting. He looked at Dr Gilbert's blade and Dr Dee's fake smile; he thought about the duke's beatings and the fear he had seen in Mary's eyes. Henry spat the liquid out as hard as he could, spraying it all over Dr Gilbert's mask and cloak.

'You think you can intimidate me with a few beatings and that stupid blade, or bribe me with these clothes?' Henry felt the veins in his neck strain as he shouted, his arms pulling against the straps that held him to the chair. 'I am from the Gap, you fools, look at the scars on my body. I have been starved and beaten my whole life. You can't force me to drink sewage and you can't make me tell you a bloody thing, Solomon be damned! Put me back in that dungeon for all I care.'

There was a slight pause and Henry felt a great release. Dr Gilbert's body jerked forward as if it had been pushed. He made a fierce, guttural grunt and with his blade raised in the air, he went to strike Henry. Dr Dee stepped across and wrestled Dr Gilbert back, pushing him off balance, but still the blade swipe only narrowly missed Henry's shoulder.

'This knave, this wretch!' Dr Gilbert bellowed and jerked forward again but Dr Dee stretched his arms out and blocked his path.

'Don't be so emotional, Gilbert,' Dr Dee said, slightly out of breath as he pushed Dr Gilbert back again. Dr Gilbert's hands dropped. He was now too far away to be able to strike Henry.

'That medicine is expensive, John. I spent days making it – it even has Venice treacle and dragon's blood in it.' Gilbert's moany tone reminded Henry of the spoiled tantrums Matthew used to throw when they were little.

'Shut up and pull yourself together,' Dr Dee shouted. He turned to look at Henry, breathing deeply to regain his composure. Stains from the medicine had rubbed off Gilbert's cloak all over Dr Dee, little beads of black powder and dribbles of liquid turning his sublime grey beard dirty as a drunkard's.

'I had hoped it would not come to this, Henry. But you leave us no choice. If the beatings can't make you co-operate, and Spanish leather shoes and a hot bath can't either, then I know of something that will.' Dr Dee paused and his eyes brightened, clearly savouring the moment. He pulled a lump of dirt from the end of his beard, rubbed it between his fingers and flicked it on to the floor. 'Gilbert, have one of the servants send for the little girl.'

Henry felt the tightness spread from his chest to every inch of his body. He realised how stupid he had been – of course they would use and abuse Mary if he did not co-operate. He could almost feel Dr Gilbert smiling through his mask as he turned and walked out of the room.

'Ok, sir, I'm sorry, I'll do as you say,' Henry pleaded with Dr Dee.

'It is too late for that now, Henry. For all I know you will change your mind again a minute later. You need to know that we will do *anything* to get the answers we require.' Dr Dee spoke calmly, as if he were giving directions to a stranger, then he took a handkerchief from his cloak and started to wipe the rest of the dirt and stains from his beard. As Henry tried to think of a way to counter, one of Graham's sayings came to him: *When you want something, always think about what's in it for the other person, always appeal to their self-interest.* Henry scoured his mind for something he could offer that would appeal to Dr Dee's self-interest, but he came up with nothing, so he just pleaded again.

'Please sir, I'll do whatever you need.'

Dr Dee stayed quiet, the silence taunting Henry. He heard footsteps coming up the stairs and the tightness in his body gripped even stronger. He hoped they had been unable to find Mary for some reason or other, but those hopes were quickly dashed.

Mary came into the room flanked by the duke's guard and Dr Gilbert. They lead her until she was stood directly in front of Henry. As if on cue, Dr Gilbert and the guard each grabbed one of Mary's arms and pulled them away from her body.

'Get off me!' Mary screamed, the chimney soot and dirt on her face making her seem all the more fierce.

'Make sure you look, Henry,' Dr Gilbert hissed. 'This is your doing. You caused this.'

'I'll co-operate, I promise! Please stop,' Henry pleaded again, wishing he'd just obeyed in the first place.

With one hand still holding Mary, the duke's guard took the nine-clawed whip from his coat and handed it to Dr Dee.

'Please, please stop, I'll do whatever you want!' Henry begged.

Dr Dee ripped open the back of Mary's dress with the same calm, methodical manner as when he spoke. There was no particular pleasure or malice in his eyes and his facial expression was empty. He may as well have been ripping up waste paper.

Mary looked into Henry's eyes and he could read so much in her expression. She was scared but she did not blame him; she was determined not to let these men crush her; she was the same Mary she had always been – feisty and ready to fight. The look reminded Henry of a group of ancient Greek philosophers he had read about called the Stoics, who advocated accepting whatever life threw at you, with valour and dignity. Mary was a Stoic. Henry tried to project strength in the look he gave back to her but he knew she could see his fear and his guilt. She stopped struggling so hard and braced herself for the beating.

'Don't worry, H, I'll be fine,' Mary said.

'Cheeky little wench,' Dr Gilbert fired back.

As Dr Dee held the whip aloft, Henry screamed.

The duke's guard was looking straight at Henry, with a satisfied tilt to his head. Dr Dee swung the whip and missed Mary's back, letting the whip come down to the floor. Henry exhaled relief.

'What are you doing, John?' Dr Gilbert shrieked. 'They need to be taught a lesson.'

Dr Dee walked over to Henry.

'Look at her,' he commanded, pointing at Mary with the whip still in his hand.

'Any time you think to disobey me, know that it is her that will pay the price.'

'Yes, sir,' Henry replied, broken.

'Get her out of my sight,' Dr Dee commanded and the men finally let go of Mary's arms. Mary quickly shot her hands behind her back and held her ripped dress together to stop it from falling off entirely and exposing her. She gave Henry a weak smile, unable to hide the fear on her face. The duke's guard escorted her out of the room.

'Now, let's start again,' Dr Dee announced, back to his chirpy self, as if nothing had ever happened.

Dr Dee asked Henry the same questions but this time, Henry carefully explained the details of his gift. They gave him another dose of medicine and Henry gulped it down. Dr Gilbert untied Henry's right arm, raised it in the air and brought his blade towards it. Henry resisted the urge to scream, clenching his teeth and pushing his legs into the ground.

Henry did not feel the cut, but he did sense the warm blood pouring from his arm. He gave in, looked and immediately felt dizzy. Dr Dee was collecting Henry's blood in a pewter bleeding bowl. Soon, the pot was full.

'Bloodletting,' Dr Dee explained, 'to keep your humours balanced. It will also allow us to see if there is something different in your blood that explains the magic.'

Dr Gilbert bandaged up Henry's arm and walked back to the desk. He passed Henry another cup filled with liquid. Henry decided not to ask what was in it this time and just drank. He felt immediately sick, burping and breathing as deeply as possible, fighting to keep his porridge down, while his head and stomach swirled.

Dr Gilbert held out a bucket in front of Henry, as if he knew what was coming, and a second later, Henry began vomiting uncontrollably. He retched and retched until all that came up was bile. His body continued to spasm, ripping at empty air trapped in his stomach.

Then, as quickly as it had come, the feeling vanished and Henry felt a strange clarity. His belly and his head felt clear and clean, as if he could suddenly inhale more air. He took deep breaths and the air even seemed to taste better. Henry noticed the scent from the flowerpots on the windowsill for the first time and the sweet aroma of the burning candles in the air.

Dr Dee handed Henry another container but it was empty. 'For you to pee in,' the doctor explained as he passed Henry another larger vessel. 'And for the other . . . Whenever you feel strong enough, the jakes is over there.' Dr Dee pointed, untying Henry's left arm.

Henry bounced up from his chair and went to walk to the washing place, but his legs almost gave way beneath him. He paused and then continued much more slowly. What was going on with his body? One second he felt stronger than ever, the next, he had the urge to fall down and sleep.

Henry made it to the washing place, did what he had to do and returned to the room with two jars, handing them to Dr Gilbert. He sat back in the seat and the doctors looked into his mouth and eyes, lifted up his arms and smelled his armpits, Dr Gilbert scribbling in his notebook the entire time.

'Henry, this shall be our final test for today,' Dr Dee said. 'We need to see your gift in action. Do you think you can manage that?'

'Just about,' Henry replied.

'That's the spirit. You'll be fine.'

Dr Gilbert helped Henry up and across the room to the desk, where a book and writing materials were waiting. More sluggish than usual, it took Henry a while, but he managed to start translating the work. It drained the last bit of energy he had.

Blood poured from Henry's arm into a bronze statue of a lion. A curved blade soared through the air but Henry blocked it with a shield. The duke stood over Henry, whip in one hand, Spanish leather shoes in the other. Henry held up his shield to protect himself. Henry's mother spoke to him, again.

'Follow him to serve your turn upon him. We cannot all be masters, nor all masters cannot truly be followed.'

163

'Henry, wake up, they want to see you,' Camilla said gently as she shook him.

Henry did not remember how he had got to bed. He rolled over and the irons dug painfully into his wrists. He did not remember when they had been put back on either.

'Ow!' he yelled. His head pounded and his throat was bone dry. 'Water please?' he asked Camilla with the tone of a beggar.

'Get up and get washed. They want to see you.'

'I need water, for Christ's sake!' Henry shrieked.

'Do not take our Lord's name in vain now, Master Henry. I must go back down and fetch the duke and his friends. If you are not ready and presentable by the time they get up here it will make me look bad. Please hurry.'

Henry desperately wanted to roll over and go back to sleep but Camilla had already put herself at risk for him – he did not want the duke to punish her because of him. In any case, the duke and the doctors now knew that they could use Mary as a weapon, any time Henry did not comply.

At the thought of Mary's scared face, Henry pulled himself up. Every movement was painful. His muscles felt as if they had been crushed between millstones and his bones were weak as twigs. Camilla helped him stumble to the washing place.

'Why did you lie for me?' Henry whispered.

'I do not know what you are talking about, Master Henry. Now please keep quiet and preserve your energy.'

Henry knew Camilla was lying.

'Ok, well, you must have your reasons so I am going to ask

you one last favour. I need to talk to Mary. Please tell her to meet me at the top of the stairs that lead down to the barn when the church bell strikes midnight.'

Camilla left without saying a word. With the irons weighing on his hands, Henry managed to wash his face and straighten himself, then stumble back to sit on the bed, despite the pain that coursed through him from head to toe.

Henry took in his surroundings. The room was smaller than the experimentation room, but it still had a proper bed. He realised it was the first time he had ever slept on anything but straw, wood or concrete. The walls were painted a plain dark blue and held two framed paintings, both depicting the same countryside scene, one hanging above a desk and chair. Henry hoped that this would be where he slept permanently from now on.

The duke and Dr Dee entered the room without knocking. With great effort Henry stood up and bowed.

'Are the manacles really still necessary, Charles?' Dr Dee asked. 'I think we managed to reach a proper understanding with Henry in the end yesterday.' Dr Dee smiled a half-gloating smile at Henry.

'You know, John, you always were too soft for your own good. This is what happens to men who never fight in a war.' Dr Dee flushed red and the duke continued. 'I agreed to have Henry in my home on one condition. If that condition should change, it will be when I decide and not a moment sooner.'

'You are quite right, Charles. I shan't mention it again. Please accept my apologies.'

The duke nodded. Looking at the duke and Dr Dee, Henry thought how cheap his own clothes were in comparison – how worn his shoes, how faded his cloak and how, where they wore silk, velvet and cotton, he wore linen and homespun wool. A day ago, he had seen all of it as rich people's clothes, but now he felt reminded he was still their social inferior. *A prisoner of such extraordinary value.*

'Good morning, Henry. I hope you are feeling a little better?' Dr Dee had his chirpy tone again. He was excited about something, Henry realised.

'A bit,' Henry lied, not wanting to admit just how weak he felt.

'Listen, Henry,' Dr Dee said, sounding more serious now. 'You did very well in those tests. I know they must have been hard, but you soldiered through. You're a strong boy.'

Dr Dee bowed to the duke as if to say, *You take over from here*, and the duke nodded in appreciation of the gesture.

The duke took a step closer and looked Henry straight in the eye. 'Listen very carefully, Henry. Tomorrow, we shall take you somewhere and you will show your gifts to a group of our friends. Do as you're told, don't embarrass us or yourself, and your life could start to become a little bit easier. If you fail to comply, you know what will happen, don't you?'

Henry thought of Mary's bare back covered with welts from the nine-clawed whip.

'Yes, sir.'

'Good. Get some rest. We have a long journey ahead of us tomorrow.'

'Yes, sir.'

'And Henry,' Dr Dee chimed in.

'Yes, sir?'

'Obedience to authority is a sign of strength, not weakness,' the doctor said, his words reminding Henry of Graham once more.

Henry could not sleep. He wondered who these friends were that the duke and the doctors were planning to take him to; he wondered how Matthew and Joan were; he wondered – as always – about his mother; but this night, it was Mary that most occupied his mind. He looked through the small window as the moon shone in and smiled. Very few slum children would ever get to sleep in a room with a glass window, let alone on an actual bed in a duke's mansion. Henry fought not to enjoy the feeling. He reminded himself that he was a prisoner in this luxury and that it would all be taken away the moment the duke had finished using him.

The church bell struck midnight and Henry's heart thumped his ribs. He got up from his bed and twisted the door handle to his room. He crept through the hallways and the kitchen, remembering the chase the duke and his guard had given them during the robbery, smiling at the thought of having trashed the duke's house. He arrived at the top of the stairs, nervous but excited. He waited; a few minutes passed. Then a few more, and still no sign of Mary. He made up a sonnet to pass the time.

A prisoner's value, a captor's will
A gift of magic? Or something stranger
In luxury's lap have I landed, still
I dream of running, despite its danger
However well fed, still a pampered pig
Fattened and seasoned, for the feast to come
I work on command, like a dancer's jig
I'll be out on me ear soon as I'm done
To run or not to run? What's the action?
To stay means hot baths and clothes of a duke
Which where I'm from are seen by a fraction
Yet if friends could see they'd surely rebuke
'Cos things can't replace the freedom I lack
So I'll find Mary and make for the Gap

Henry leaned up against a wall and felt himself start to fall asleep. If he did not go back to his room now, he'd fall asleep right on this spot. Only half-disappointed, Henry pulled himself up and walked back to his room. Climbing into his bed, looking at the moonlit sky, he was already having doubts about running away from all of this.

The general takes one of the strangers as his new wife,

a beautiful noblewoman by the name of Desdemona.

But the general is not lucky in love; Eshu is upon him.

12

The horse moved beneath him and Henry panicked that something was going to smash him in the face. Blindfolded, he slowly adapted to his new lack of sight, and tuned into his other senses. He listened to the patter of hooves and could tell that the duke's horse was just a little further ahead but still, it was scary to be riding alone and blindfolded. Every so often, he felt the tension as the rope that tied his horse to the duke's became taut and jolted him. Henry felt as if he could fall at any moment.

The song of a light wind told him they were in a wide open space, then changes in sounds and smells suggested they had entered a forest. The scent of berries and leaves and honey and moisture, the buzz of bees, the flitting of flies, the scurrying of squirrels, the whistles of birds – they all sang out to Henry with a clarity he never experienced when he was able to use his eyes.

He felt the forest clearing, its sounds replaced by the melody of lightly running water. As he heard the horse's hooves splash through the stream, Henry felt the vibrations from the stones at the bottom reverberate through the animal's bones and body and into him. It was a strange sensation, like the music of nature was playing within him.

They began to climb a steep hill. Henry squeezed with

everything his thighs and mid-section could muster so to feel safe. He tried to imagine what the surrounding landscape looked like, picturing the rocky stream and the forest down below and the green hills he was now climbing. He tasted the air – it was sweet and crisp.

'Riding blindfolded is part of everyone's initiation. You'd be surprised how many men fall off.' The duke had not spoken the entire journey and the sound of his voice made Henry jump.

'Why?' Henry asked.

'Why what?'

'Why choose riding blindfolded for an initiation?'

'Obviously because we don't want any new initiates knowing where we are before they can be trusted. But also because sight and vision are not the same thing, young man. To acquire true knowledge and wisdom, a man must be able to look into himself and not just out into the world.'

There it is again, Henry thought. The thoughtful duke, the rich man with the palace who had dedicated his fortune to building a great library when he could afford all the jewels and doxies in the world. The man who truly loved his family. *How could this same man be so brutal and so cold?*

They came to a stop and Henry could hear the duke climbing down from his horse. He felt a touch on his leg. 'Pass me your hand.' The duke spoke in a new way and Henry could not quite tell what his tone meant.

The duke helped Henry to the ground. He placed his hand on Henry's back and gently pushed, ushering him to walk. 'This way, Henry. Watch out for the steps and feel for the wall.'

Henry put his hands out in front of him and then to the left and the right, finding a rugged stone wall that was pleasantly coarse beneath his fingers. Through the darkness he inched his feet forward until he felt his toe overhang a step.

'There you go, that's the first one. Hold on to the wall with one hand and put the other on my shoulder.' The duke moved Henry's hand into place.

Henry realised what was new about the duke's voice – he was not used to serving anyone, let alone the likes of Henry. He was still trying to sound firm, yet it was impossible when helping a blindfolded boy down a flight of stairs. Instead, his voice was helpful, affectionate even.

Their shoes clattered on the stone, and Henry smiled, savouring the sound their heels made – strong and sturdy, nothing like the rotten cloth that he had worn for shoes his whole life.

They climbed down steps for at least five minutes. Henry tried to imagine how deep below ground they were. He went to step down again and nearly tripped – the ground was flat suddenly.

'Forgive me,' the duke said, with a hint of playful laughter. 'No more steps here.'

He guided Henry through a tight corridor – he could hear how close the walls were – and Henry felt claustrophobic even though he could not see.

'A few upwards steps coming,' the duke warned.

Henry felt forward with his toe, found the step and climbed the short staircase. He heard a door open before him and the sounds changed again as he walked through. He could tell that the walls here were wooden and not stone. They crossed another room and through another doorway and then another. He heard the duke knock at a door.

'Know thyself. To seek eternal wisdom,' shouted a voice from inside.

Henry gaped in shock at the words as the duke replied, 'Look within to the only true kingdom.'

He had never thought to ask Joan if their secret incantation was in fact secret; he had just assumed it was. He did not know whether to feel disappointed or intrigued that these elite men were using it too.

As Henry entered he could feel the heat of many bodies. He heard breathing and mumbles, and the smell of drinks and tobacco. He reckoned the room must have had at least ten or fifteen people in it.

Someone pushed Henry towards a seat and Henry sat. He felt a hand at the back of his head as the blindfold was removed. Henry blinked as he looked around the room: there were about twenty men sitting around a large table, and all clearly nobles or notables of some kind, dressed and bejewelled in satins and silks, ruffs and doublets with gold embroidery and rings encrusted with coloured stones.

Henry spotted Dr Dee among the men and wondered if Dr Gilbert was there too. As he scanned the room he saw a man with neck-length curly hair and a bald patch at the front of his head. He would recognise that face anywhere; he had seen it on stage so many times.

William Shakespeare.

He had never had the desire to impress someone as much as he wanted to impress Shakespeare. The great playwright and poet was his inspiration, the reason why he wrote sonnets like he did. To be in the same room as Mr William Shakespeare was like all Henry's dreams coming true at once. Henry felt a nervous rush. His hands went clammy and his heart rate quickened.

The men stared at Henry with the same look in their eyes that Dr Dee and Dr Gilbert had when they'd first visited him in the cell. Henry guessed they had all been told about his gift but would not believe it until they saw it for themselves.

The men stood up and crowded around Henry, all the while keeping a slight distance. Henry could not tell if that spoke of fear, fascination or disgust.

The duke lit some frankincense in an ornate golden bowl and waved it around the room, filling the air with a thin smoke. Henry took a deep breath, the refreshing aroma filling his lungs.

'Gentlemen of the council,' Dr Dee began. 'This here' – he nodded at Henry – 'is the young Moor whom Charles has been telling us of. Dr Gilbert and myself have been testing his miraculous gifts, trying to understand them.'

As Dr Dee spoke, Henry took in the room, which seemed to be both a large study and a gentlemen's club. Aside from the main table, there were several wooden desks. A few cushioned chairs were dotted around and bookshelves were scattered across the room, some bending round corners and embedded into the waxed wooden walls, others jutting out and straight. A two-person table held an oak chess-board that was set, ready to play, its pieces made of gold and silver. To Henry's right was a small cupboard displaying glasses as well as silver and gold vessels. The glasses themselves were engraved with shapes and coats of arms. Henry could also see that the room was connected to several smaller adjacent rooms.

How in the hell did they build this so far underground? Henry wondered.

'His gifts will speed up our work here immeasurably,' Dr Dee continued. 'It gives me great delight to introduce to you our newest friend and seeker, Henry White.'

The men laughed and Dr Dee winked at Henry with a playful smile. It was an odd practice, giving a black person the name 'White' – a joke that the men seemed to find really funny. Henry had heard stories of a famous black trumpet player who used to play at the court of Henry VII and was known as John Blanke. It seemed the joke had caught on since then.

Henry smiled as if he found the joke funny, but inside he boiled with fury.

'So, Henry, time to show our friends here what you can do,' Dr Dee announced.

The duke laid the usual tools on the desk in front of Henry – a text, a blank notebook, an inkpot and quills. The room had no windows of course, but candleholders were dotted every few feet along the walls, each with a candle aflame inside it. In addition, four black metal chandeliers hung from the ceiling, each with at least twenty candles. They reminded Henry of giant spiders' legs.

Henry stared at the tools on the desk. He dared not look across the room at Shakespeare again, for fear of stage fright. Instead, he opened the book, placed his hand over the first page and closed his eyes. With his right hand he picked up the quill. He knew he had to do this, if he wanted any chance of seeing Mary, Joan or Matthew ever again.

It took a moment to clear his head, but when the colours came, they shone with a burning brightness. Henry's quill started to move rapidly. Even in his state he could hear the shocked mutterings of the men around him as they read back the words Henry was writing.

'Maybe he just knows this text off by heart. This could simply be an exercise of memory,' one man said. The comment jolted Henry out of his trance.

'Ay, you pick a book. Language of your choosing.' Henry's words came almost as a reflex.

'Well! The Moor's got more than dormouse valour, hasn't he?' someone exclaimed and all the men laughed, coughing clouds of tobacco smoke into the air.

Henry looked to Shakespeare, hoping to see approval or admiration.

All he found was a blank stare that he could not read.

'Well?' The duke gazed around the room, offering the challenge to the nay-sayers.

'As a matter of fact, I have one from Cathay that has been puzzling my translators for many years,' someone said. He took a worn manuscript out of his bag and tossed it on to the table in front of Henry.

Henry recognised the writing. It was the same as one of the books he had tried to steal from the duke's library. *So I was right – it was from Cathay.*

Henry moved the first text and put the new one in its place, laying his hand over the first page. The whole process began again, Henry's quill furiously scribbling as the colours shaped and morphed into letters in his mind. The man who'd given him the text read the sentence Henry was writing aloud.

*The Tao that can be named is not the eternal Tao
Naming is the origin of all particular things.*

Silence descended on the room as Henry continued to scribble at a frantic pace, turning page after page until he had completed the entire text.

'What witchcraft is this?' one of the men shouted.

'More like a gift from God,' someone shouted back, 'and I don't even believe in him.'

Most of the men laughed at this blasphemy but Henry saw one cross himself and mutter words to the Lord begging forgiveness. He just knew that this was Dr Gilbert without his mask, though he was surprised. Dr Gilbert looked much more like his voice than the person Henry had imagined. He had a round babyface, smooth skin and the eyes of an infant. No pockmarks, no shrivelled skin and nothing that really gave any indication of his hard attitude. Henry half-wondered if he covered his face during treatments so that people would take him more seriously.

Henry could see the astonishment on many of the men's faces, but he could also tell that some still thought it was a kind of trick at play – not just from the way they were looking at him, but the way they were glancing at the duke too.

The duke placed his hands on Henry's shoulders as if he were his property. 'As you can see, Henry's abilities will enhance the nature of our work quite dramatically. I for one think we should all take a toast to that.'

Everyone, even the nay-sayers, picked up their glasses and raised them.

'To Lord Wilmslow and his Moor, Henry White,' Dr Dee said.

'To Wilmslow and White,' everybody repeated and swigged from their glasses.

Dr Dee even poured Henry a glass. 'Drink up, my boy,' he encouraged Henry, patting him on the back so enthusiastically that Henry almost spilled his wine.

Henry took a sip. *His Moor, his Moor?* he said to himself, smiling through the irritation.

As the formal meeting finished, everyone except Shakespeare

crowded closer around Henry and badgered him with questions about his gift.

'Where did you learn this witchcraft?'

'How do you do it?'

'Can you teach others?'

'What did you have to give up in exchange for this magic?'

Question after question. One of the men even asked Henry if he could touch his hair. It felt a little like an interrogation, but still, Henry did his best to answer them, hearing the curiosity, envy and fascination in each voice. Dr Gilbert's words echoed in his head again. *A prisoner of such extraordinary value.* It was hard not to feel important with all this attention.

But Henry was also uneasy. He felt a bit like a circus performer, a wild exotic bird, *the duke's Moor*, the poor orphan with the special gift. These men would not have noticed him in a thousand lifetimes ordinarily, and were only interested in him because of what he could do for them. Yet Henry could not deny that it still felt good to be admired by men of such importance. Back in the Gap nobody really appreciated the fact that Henry could read; other boys even made fun of him for reading, calling him a 'pretend noble'. Though Henry's fists could always put a stop to the name-calling, Henry realised he had never met a man that he could spar with intellectually. Sure, Graham was wise in a village-elder kind of a way, but he could not discuss Plato, Aristotle and Avicenna. For the first time in Henry's life, he was surrounded by men that respected and admired him because he was smart. But they were also heartless nobles.

Henry looked up and saw Shakespeare sitting alone at one of the desks across the room, writing away in his notebook, smoking his pipe and drinking his wine, uninterested in Henry or any of the kerfuffle. The bitter-sweet feelings dug deeper. Clearly, he hadn't impressed the one man whose opinion mattered most to him.

The girl is now a young woman.

She enters the general's bedchamber to find her father

and his new wife dead.

Fearing how the strangers would react to the death of one of

their own, the young woman runs from the lands of the Doge.

A new boat, another shore, more prayers to Olokun,

God of the oceans.

The duke, Dr Dee and Dr Gilbert were sitting at the far end of the duke's huge dining table. It was made of solid oak, as were the chairs, which each held a fine silk-covered cushion, and delicately carved geometric patterns around the top of its seatback. Henry was not sure if he should approach or not. The duke's guard was standing by the wall and Camilla's children were scurrying in and out of the kitchen carrying trays of food. Henry had heard all sorts of rules for banqueting at the home of a noble, but he had never imagined he'd need to recall them.

Dining with nobles or at the queen's court?
Men without rank should sit below the salt.

Henry remembered the rhyme and scanned the table for the salt cellar.

'Have a seat, Henry,' the duke offered.

Henry sat two seats down from the salt cellar. He decided he could not sit right at the end, as the men would have to shout to talk to him on a table this big, but he was still eight seats from where the duke and the doctors were sitting.

'Very good,' Dr Dee said. 'Maybe you have some breeding after all.'

The smells coming from the kitchen and the covered pots on the table turned Henry's stomach and mouth to water. He could smell spiced meats and roasted carrots, turnips and sweet things. He could hardly concentrate on the men's faces for hunger.

'You did well yesterday, Henry,' the duke said.

'Very well,' Dr Dee added.

The duke gestured to his guard, who walked towards Henry, took a key out of his pocket and removed his manacles. Henry started to turn and stretch his wrists, but quickly stopped when he realised it could be taken as rude.

'Am I going to live to regret that decision, Henry?' the duke asked.

'No, sir.'

'Good. So here are the new rules. You can live without manacles. You shall work for us, translating and answering any questions we might have. You will contribute to discussions as and when you are asked to do so. I will have a desk put into your room and plenty of supplies so you can begin as soon as possible. We have a huge backlog of foreign texts, actually.'

'Quite,' Dr Dee chimed in.

'In exchange for this work, you shall receive your room, board and clothes – grace for grace. But you are never to disobey me, boy. Do you understand?'

'Yes, sir,' Henry said.

'Very good.'

Mary and one of Camilla's children came into the room

carrying a turkey on a platter. Henry tried to catch her eye as Mary put the turkey on the table, but she did not meet his gaze.

Camilla's husband came into the dining hall and began to slice the turkey, setting down a piece for each of the men. Before he'd cut a piece for Henry, he went to open another tray. Henry feared it was more torture than he could take to sit here and watch the men eat all this glorious food without so much as a taste.

'What about Henry?' the duke asked.

'Oh.' There was obvious resentment in Camilla's husband's voice. 'I did not realise the Moor was eating too, sir.'

'Well, he is, so serve him,' the duke commanded.

Henry saw Camilla's husband catch himself before he said anything else, instead pursing his lips and cutting Henry a piece of turkey.

The man moved on to other meats that Henry did not recognise. One was a dark-brown round loaf with parsley sprinkled over it and mint sauce on the side. Another looked a bit like chicken and was stuffed with sage and onions. One looked bloody and soft, only delicately cooked on the outside. There were several kinds of fish too, decorated with lemons and oranges and a shrivelled black fruit that Henry had never seen before. The children served out small portions of roasted carrots and parsnips and it was all Henry could do to restrain himself from digging his face straight into his plate.

'Dr Gilbert, would you do us the honour of saying grace?' the duke asked.

'Of course, sir, I'd be delighted.' The men closed their eyes and clasped their hands, as did the servants standing at the side of the room. Henry followed suit.

'*Pater noster, qui es in caelis, sanctificetur nomen tuum . . .*' Dr Gilbert started off the Lord's Prayer in Latin as to be expected. But he did not do the usual version of the Prayer that was only a few lines long. He mixed in other random parts of the Bible and added in his own reflections, meandering along while the hot meat steamed up into Henry's nostrils, driving him wild.

Eventually, the duke gave a polite cough to let Dr Gilbert know it was time to finish.

'Amen,' Dr Gilbert concluded, and the men started eating.

Henry went to grab his knife but there was another utensil on the other side of his plate that Henry had never seen before. All the men were using it to eat along with their knife and Henry wondered how to mimic what they were doing. It seemed so unusual.

'It's called a fork, Henry,' Dr Dee said, and Henry felt himself blush. He must have noticed Henry staring. 'Old Wilmslow here is far too cultured for us peasants.' Dr Dee laughed. 'He thinks everything they do in Italy should be brought to England. But don't worry, we only use them when we are here. Charles insists that it's uncultured to eat with just a knife in this day and age.'

'It is,' the duke said, taking a big gulp of wine into his meat-filled mouth.

'You just cut your meat and stab it with the fork, like this.'

The duke demonstrated. 'It makes eating so much easier.'

Henry cut and then piled his fork with turkey, several other meats and a carrot. He wanted to shout out loud with pleasure as he placed it in his mouth; the creamy carrots were coated in butter and the meats were soft and smooth. As for the shrivelled black fruit, it was as sweet as sugar and made the fish taste heavenly.

'Fetch the salt,' the duke ordered.

Mary placed the tray she was carrying on the table and walked towards Henry to fetch the salt, but still she did not meet his eye. As she sprinkled some salt on to the duke's plate, Henry could not suppress the strange feeling as he watched her. Here he was, sat at the table with the duke and his friends as if he were a noble and Mary was their servant. It did not feel right, but what could he do?

'By your patience, good sirs. Can Mary join us?' Henry asked the duke.

From the way Mary whipped her head around to glare at him, Henry knew he had made a stupid mistake.

The duke and the other men laughed – even the duke's guard, though he still stood at the side of the room and was not eating himself. Henry could see Mary fighting down her embarrassment and felt so annoyed with himself.

''Tis not my household of course, but may I do our gracious duke a favour and take the floor?' Dr Dee asked, looking smug.

The duke nodded.

'Henry, if you are to become a man of any rank, even lowly,'

Dr Dee began, 'you must understand what rank means. You, by virtue of your unique gifts, are able to make yourself useful to men of power, men of quality and means and influence. Do not take this for granted. You owe your seat at this table and even your very life to this fact. For what reason should this girl be allowed to dine with us?'

Dr Dee looked to Henry as if there were a suitable answer and Henry felt himself shaking. He could not believe he would not even use Mary's name.

'Simply because she is your annoying little cousin?' Dr Dee continued. 'She is lucky not to be a Newgate nightingale and behind bars. If all men of quality were to eat with those born to serve us, what next? May as well invite our horses to join us at dinner too.'

Dr Gilbert raised his glass. 'Quite right,' he said and the duke raised his glass too.

Henry looked down and played with his cutlery. He could not bear to see the look on Mary's face. He took another sip of wine and a bite of his steak. He could feel Mary standing obediently at the side of the room but still he did not look up.

'Do you understand, Henry?' Dr Dee asked.

'Yes, sir, I understand,' Henry replied, feeling utterly stupid as he finally looked up. It was now that really he noticed Mary's clothes. She was dressed in a clean-ish version of the same cheap cloth that they had worn their whole lives, as were all the other servants, except Camilla's husband, who had the dignity of a clean pair of breeches and a cheap shirt. They also wore aprons and cooking gloves, their heads sweating from their work to make this meal and from marching in and out of the kitchen with the feast. Mary would have seemed ridiculously out of place if she'd sat at the table with them wearing her serving clothes.

Nobles are an odd bunch, Henry thought. They liked to dress up their pages in fine clothes to show just how rich they were – so rich they could afford to dress their servants like miniature nobles if they wanted to. But they also took pleasure in just how cruelly and poorly they could treat the rest of the help. They'd give the best scraps from their plates to their dogs before they let the kitchen hands or cleaners have them. Henry already knew all this well from the tales of the kitchen hands and cooks that lived in the Gap, but seeing it first-hand was something else.

What were you thinking, Henry, you jolt-head?

'You see, rank comes from God almighty himself,' Dr Gilbert said. 'As god is to man, so man is to woman and so rich is to poor.'

Over the next few weeks, then months as autumn turned to winter, Henry only really saw Mary at mealtimes. Every time shame washed over him. Mary reminded him of how much he was lying to himself. Mary could surely see how absurd it was for Henry to be dressed in these fine clothes, sat at the table of one of the wealthiest dukes in England.

He knew that Mary still slept in the barn with the other servants, which added to his guilt. His room had a proper bed, and even its own washbasin. He had a cloak, four shirts, six pairs of breeches, two nether socks, three ruffs and a pair of Spanish leather shoes. What Mary wore was a glorified potato sack. He had a desk and a chair with back support. Mary probably did not sit down from sun up to sun down. She, Camilla and Camilla's children served breakfast, lunch and dinner, washed the dishes, scrubbed the floors and even cleaned up after the duke's horses – the horses being better fed and cared for than they were.

Henry spent all day doing what he loved: translating, reading and making notes on particular subjects of the duke's choosing. It was at night-time that the guilt really hit him, as he tried to sleep in his comfortable bed and thought about Mary and Camilla asleep on the straw in the barn, with the flies and the smell and the horses. He thought about how Camilla had lied for him and the way Mary had screamed with concern when she saw his skinny body after a week in the dungeon. He felt like the ultimate coward. He wondered if Joan was all right and what had happened to Matthew. He tried to push the thoughts from his mind, but every night they returned to meddle with his sleep.

Yet Henry grew used to his new reality. As the winter months passed, the feelings of guilt started to subside. Twice a week, Henry was blindfolded and taken on the horse, and each time it felt just as new, just as dangerous and just as magical as the first. Twice a week he descended those stone steps, his hand on the duke's shoulder, and wound his way through the wooden corridors, until he knew he could navigate them unassisted if he had to. Some days he would just translate for the council; other days they would discuss the latest theories or ideas, and sometimes they each took turns to read stories from the farthest corners of the globe.

For the first time in his life Henry felt that he was part of history, that he could affect the world in some way. After all, here he was among some of the most educated men in England, part of a secret council of artists, clergymen, physicians, politicians and intellectuals, exchanging thoughts and ideas, translating priceless books from all across the globe and debating questions that most were forbidden to even entertain. He even stopped flinching at being called Henry White. There was an affection to it, like any good nickname. And he was *the duke's Moor* after all, wasn't he? He was like one of the great thinkers of history he'd read about, pursuing knowledge regardless of the consequences.

The stone table was large and round. In its centre the sun was painted with the circulating signs of the zodiac. The iron chairs were welded into the floor. Henry knew who all of the people sat at the table were, despite having never seen their faces before. Imhotep, Hammurabi, Plato, Lao Tzu, Ashvaghosa, Hypatia of Alexandria, Ahmed Baba, Leonardo da Vinci, the Hogon of the Dogon, Pachamama of the

Andes, Averroes, Aristotle and Juan Latino. A conversation was raging among these great sages about the nature of reality, the origins of life and death and the limits of human knowledge. They had been at this table having this same conversation since the beginning of time, Henry knew that now, though he would not know it later. He stood far away at the end of a great hall observing and listening to the conversation. Next to him stood his mother and Shakespeare, while across the other side of the room stood the duke and the two doctors, all of them watching the table. Every so often Henry would notice that one of the people at the table had become someone else – Plato was now a woman of the Sioux, Hamurabi had given way to Michelangelo, Shango sat where Averroes had just been – but the conversation did not stop.

When Henry awoke he remembered nothing.

The general's daughter tries again to make her way.

This time in London, land of Elizabeth.

'Good day, sirs.' Henry tipped his hat as the duke and Dr Dee walked past him and across the cobblestone courtyard, past the water fountain, and climbed into the horse-drawn carriage.

The duke's carriage was large enough to seat at least four to six people, judging by the outside, with finely curved edges and swirling gold patterns of artwork that contrasted with its onyx black exterior. Its wheels were almost as tall as Henry himself.

The duke and Dr Dee sat themselves in the carriage and Henry turned to walk back inside the house.

'What are you waiting for, Henry? You are going to make us late,' the duke shouted.

'Pardon, sir.' Henry hoped he had heard right, but did not dare to presume just yet.

'Hurry up and get in. We don't have all day!'

Though he could not see the duke, Henry could hear him smile through his words. Henry had to stop himself from skipping towards the carriage as he thought about how much he'd always wanted to ride in one. Not only that, but they were going to see Shakespeare's new play – he had heard them talk about it at dinner. Henry felt the look of resentment from the duke's guard, who was sat at the front, exposed to the elements. Henry smiled inside, just a bit.

Henry jumped in and closed the door and off they went. The duke and Dr Dee talked but Henry paid little attention. He was far too preoccupied with taking in the experience – the feeling of moving without having to do anything. It was almost like magic.

The ride was much bumpier than being on horseback, though the seat was far more comfortable than a saddle. Henry spent the journey peering through the window of the carriage, observing the people outside on foot. Heads turned as they rolled by. People were trying to get a glimpse of who was inside. Henry could see them, but they could not see him through the curtains. He remembered doing the same himself as carriages had rolled past.

As they crossed London Bridge, Henry looked around at all the spots where he had picked a pocket. His life could have been so different if he had been caught by anyone else but Wilmslow. *You've come a long way, lad*, he said to himself, hearing Graham's voice in his head. Henry missed the old man.

They pulled up at the Globe near a few other carriages. Henry got out first and held the door for Dr Dee and the duke. They walked to the front of the queue and went straight in through the expensive entrance. The people in the normal queue looked at them as if to say, *Who are they?* Henry thought about how many times he had done the same, relishing the feeling of importance those envious looks gave him.

'Good afternoon, sirs,' a page boy said, lighting a lantern as he spoke. He guided them up the dark stairwell and across the balcony to a private box overlooking the stage. The best seats in the house. From here they could see the whole stage without a single body in their way and, more importantly, they could also be seen by everybody else, including the actors. The box was larger than the house Henry had grown up in and screamed one thing: wealth.

'Good afternoon, sirs,' a pretty serving-maid said as they entered the box. 'Would you care for wine or beer, or something stronger?'

I could get used to this, Henry thought. He had never been called sir in his life, and now he had been called it twice in five minutes. *Sir Henry White has a nice Shakespearean ring to it.*

'Wine for the boy, brandy for the men,' the duke declared as they took their seats. Henry tried not to be annoyed by that word again – 'boy'.

The trumpets sounded to signal the start of the play. Henry looked out over the audience and remembered all those times he had gazed up at the wealthy people, dreaming that one day he would be the one up there. And here he was in that elevated place, a cushion sewn into the back of his seat and a beautiful young woman pouring his wine. He looked at the groundlings and saw just how dirty and gaunt they were, how rowdy and unrefined their behaviour and how their hundreds of sweaty, unwashed bodies smelled so terribly. They gave the theatre a musty tinge despite its open-air roof. No wonder some of the nobles in the other boxes covered their noses with lemons or oranges.

Henry swirled the wine in his glass and slowly sniffed it before taking a sip. He almost laughed out loud at himself as he realised he was imitating the ways of the nobility, and how quickly and automatically it had happened. If only Moll Cutpurse and the old gang could see him now: leather stampers on his feet, sniffing and sipping wine in his private box, looking down on the groundlings with disgust.

But this flicker of pride left him feeling cold with embarrassment.

Henry's attention returned to the play. There were just two actors on stage. The star of the show playing Prince Hamlet looked about the same age as Henry. The other actor was wrapped head to toe in a white sheet with a king's crown on top, playing the ghost of Hamlet's recently murdered father.

'*Speak. I am bound to hear,*' Hamlet said to his father's ghost.

'*So art thou to revenge, when thou shalt hear,*' the actor said from beneath the sheet as he moved away across the stage.

'*What?*' Hamlet shouted after him, the look on his face one of genuine fear and confusion.

'*I am thy father's spirit,*

Doomed for a certain term to walk the night.'

The audience were so silent you could almost hear them breathing. Henry looked at the ghost of Hamlet's father and thought about his own mother and his dreams about her. *Do the dreams mean she is dead?* Henry wondered.

The ghost continued, his voice pounding across the arena like the drums in the bear pit.

> *'I am forbid*
> *To tell the secrets of my prison house,*
> *I could a tale unfold whose lightest word*
> *Would harrow up thy soul, freeze thy young blood,*
> *Make thy two eyes, like stars, start from their spheres.'*

As the play went on, Henry thought about his family history, the curse, his mother's reasons for leaving.

> *'Taint not thy mind, nor let thy soul contrive*
> *Against thy mother aught. Leave her to heaven*
> *And to those thorns that in her bosom lodge*
> *To prick and sting her.'*

It was like the ghost was talking directly to Henry. What should he do? Should he forgive his mother for leaving him? Punish her? How could he punish a woman he'd probably never meet? And even though she'd never been in his life it had always felt as if she was trying to guide and protect him through his dreams. How would heaven judge her?

> *'Adieu, adieu. Remember me.'*

The ghost left the stage and Henry wondered what his

mother would want him to do. What did his dreams mean? How could he ever really understand them?

The play finished and a silence came over the audience.

Maybe the groundlings did not get it. None of them can read. It probably went over their heads. But the looks on their faces suggested something quite different . . .

Then, as if they had heard Henry's thoughts, the applause began and the crowd cheered. It was clear that they too felt as if they had just witnessed something very special. Calls started for the encore.

'Shall we leave?' the duke said as if it were a question, yet he and Dr Dee had already got out of their seats. Henry wanted to tell him he would like to stay for the encore, but he knew well enough that he was being commanded. And Henry had learned from conversations at the dinner table that the nobility considered the encore to be a lowly form of entertainment performed solely for the rabble down below. To stay would be seen as the height of bad taste for a man of the duke's quality.

Henry got up and took one last look over the balcony, trying to imagine himself back among those groundlings with whom he had stood shoulder to shoulder countless times.

He knew in his heart that he did not fit down there any more.

They emerged from the theatre back on to Bankside, where Dr Dee tipped his hat.

'I must depart,' he said and disappeared up the street.

Henry and the duke walked towards the carriage. The duke's

guard was talking to a lady of about the duke's age. Her long red hair complemented her skin; skin that was somehow pale and glowing at the same time. The duke's eyes lit up when he saw her and Henry noticed the subtle change in the speed of his walk.

A group of younger women stood a few feet away. Henry could tell they must be connected to the older woman from the similar style of their clothes – long finely crafted dresses, bejewelled necks and wrists, and quality shoes. Yet not one of them had the aura of nobility, and of course no noblewoman would come to the theatre without her husband or a male servant in attendance, lest the rumour mill start.

Among them Henry fixated on one girl in particular. She was so beautiful it was almost painful. She had a tanned complexion with skin that looked so healthy Henry knew that she could not be a Londoner. Her long brown hair cascaded down her back in thick ringlets and even through her dress Henry could tell she had the kind of strong, sturdy legs that men craved. Her eyes were of the same deep brown as the wood that lined a brand-new ship and Henry tried to imagine where she might have come from. He felt himself staring, but as hard as he tried to look away, he simply could not command his eyes to do so.

'Henry.'

'Henry.'

'Henry!'

It was only the annoyance in the duke's tone that shook Henry from his daydream.

'Yes, sir,' he replied, feeling panicked. Henry saw the duke and the older woman chuckle at him and the duke whispered something into her ear.

'Lucia,' the older woman called, beckoning the beautiful young girl to come over.

Lucia. What a perfect name, Henry thought.

She walked towards them and Henry fought to keep his breath under control.

'You are not a man yet, are you, boy?' the duke said to Henry, nudging him as they both watched Lucia walk.

'No, sir,' Henry replied.

The duke smirked.

'Lucia, this is Henry.' The older woman grabbed Lucia's right hand as she spoke. 'And Henry, this is Lucia.' She took Henry's hand and joined it to Lucia's. Henry almost melted at the softness of Lucia's skin.

'You two lovebirds have a good time,' the older woman said.

'Listen, Henry,' the duke said in a more serious tone. 'I have some business of my own to attend to, so I shall see you in the morning. Lucia knows where to bring you. Don't do anything stupid.' The duke looked to Lucia, and Henry could read what the glance was saying: *Don't you let him do anything stupid either*.

'Yes, sir,' Henry replied.

'Good, well, enjoy yourself and I will see you tomorrow.' And with that, the duke and the red-haired woman hopped into his carriage and the horses trotted off.

Southwark suddenly didn't seem so scary to Henry as he

walked with Lucia along the riverbank. The drunks and the thieves, the beggars and the street children were still lurking, but they were no longer important. How could they be when Henry was staring into the most beautiful face he'd ever seen?

The afternoon sun slowly faded over St Paul's, turning the London sky summer-red. Lucia smiled and Henry imagined London to be like Florence or Paris – or some other romantic city that he'd read about – rather than the den of thieves and killers he'd known all these years.

'So, where are you from, Lucia?' Henry asked, breaking the ice.

'I come from Venice,' Lucia stated. There was a quiet dignity to the way she said the word *Venice*; one that Henry had come to expect from people that hailed from that proud republic.

Henry paused and Lucia spoke again, a concerned sweetness filling her broken English. 'You all right, Henry?'

'Yeah, it's just . . . my mum is from Venice, well, *was* . . . I mean, she lived there for a long time.'

'Oh . . . is she . . . ?'

'No, she's not dead,' Henry said, then paused again. 'Actually, I'm not sure.' He did not know if he was ready to tell his life story to a complete stranger.

They stopped by a pile of broken barrels. Henry picked up a pebble and threw it into the Thames with great force, watching the stone skim across the water and create miniature ponds of ripples. He picked up another stone and threw it as he spoke. 'I don't know if my mother is dead or alive. She left me as a child. I was raised by her friend, Joan.'

Lucia looked closer into Henry's face. 'My mother die when I born. My father, I don't know.' The intensity in her eyes scared Henry slightly, as if she was staring into his fears, hopes and dreams and Henry could not close himself up to stop her.

'So who raised you?' Henry asked. He could see Lucia thinking, searching for the words.

'Church,' she said, then rubbed her fingers the way people always seemed to do when looking for a word, as if their hands could pull words from the air. 'Church men, but lady.'

Henry thought about what this could mean. 'Nuns?' he asked, throwing another pebble into the water.

'*Bene*.'

'You were raised in a nunnery?'

'*Bene*, but I run.' Lucia looked away from Henry. 'The nun not nice, the man even worse.'

'Sooth,' Henry said. Lucia stepped closer to Henry. Henry copied the movement and put his arm round her. They glanced at each other awkwardly and eventually Henry plucked up the courage to lean in.

'Henry!'

The voice calling his name was loud and familiar but it still took Henry a moment to place it. He turned around, seeing the crowds of groundlings pouring out of the theatre; the encore must have finished. Among them Henry saw Mary, Camilla and Camilla's daughters. Instantly Henry felt embarrassed and he hated himself for it, but as he scanned their clothes he could not help but think about how awful they looked.

Mary came closer. She looked at Lucia with no offer of friendship in her eyes, and Lucia looked Mary up and down with the kind of disgusted look nobles often had when they accidentally had to walk through the slums. Mary suddenly seemed older, somehow.

Henry did not know what to do. He wanted to be happy to see Mary, but why did she have to be here now, of all times?

'Hello,' Mary said to Henry, though she was cutting her eye at Lucia again. 'How are you doing?' Mary came closer and went to hug Henry but he stepped back automatically, looking down at his clean expensive clothes.

Mary glanced at her dirty dress and smiled uncomfortably. 'Oh, ay,' she said. The sweet shame in her acceptance that she was too dirty to hug him stung Henry more than an open insult.

'Who is this doxy anyway?' she asked, her tone changed, pointing at Lucia without looking her way.

'Don't be so rude, Mary,' Henry replied.

'Since when was the truth rude?' Mary shot back.

'You her know?' Lucia asked Henry. Even with her limited English she knew how to put anger into her voice.

'The doxy can't even speak English properly,' Mary said and laughed.

Lucia raised her hands and went to walk away. 'I leave you, her.' She gestured to Henry and then to Mary.

'No, Lucia, wait! It's fine,' Henry said, grabbing Lucia's arm.

'She's just my annoying little cousin.'

As soon as the words left his mouth Henry regretted them. The colour drained from Mary's face and the feisty lioness turned into a meek wounded cat in an instant. Henry could see how hard Mary was fighting back the tears, her lip quivering as she tried to speak. Henry wanted to apologise, because he knew that was what he was supposed to do, but as he looked at Mary, run-down and dirty, with torn clothes and ragged shoes, he just felt annoyed. Why had she intruded in his new life and showed him a picture of his former self?

Mary turned and walked back to Camilla and her daughters without saying a word. Even though Camilla was a little too far way to have heard what was said, Henry could tell from the way she looked at him that she had read the whole scenario.

Lucia linked her arm to Henry's. 'We go,' she said, her tone sensual and persuasive.

Henry watched Mary and Camilla walk off and could not chase after her, despite the guilt he felt. Being with Lucia was far more important to him. Mary would always be there. Lucia he might never see again.

'So, what is Venice like?' Henry asked, desperate to know. He thought of the wonderful tales he had heard – the grandeur of its buildings, the magical floating city, a land of abundance and wealth.

'Like London,' she replied. Henry was almost hurt by the derisive tone in her voice.

'What? How?'

'If you have money, Venice is great. If you poor, you starve or you die or you beg or you steal – or if you woman . . .' Lucia trailed off. 'But . . . boy do this too, just like London.'

They walked in silence for a moment, Henry taken aback by the bitter tone of Lucia's voice when she talked about her hometown. 'So why did you come to Romeville?'

'I just go. I run from nun and then I run from Venice. I hear London good – school and hospital for poor children, woman for king. I come.'

'Would you ever go back?'

Lucia paused before answering. 'If I rich, yes. Rich, I show them, but poor, no . . . poor, I stay here.' She laughed and gazed at Henry. 'You and duke . . . why?'

Henry translated Lucia's broken words in his mind. 'Well, London . . . it's like you said – if you poor, you steal or starve . . . I steal.' Henry realised he had started to speak in Lucia's broken English but he couldn't stop it. 'I steal in duke house, but I get caught. Now I must pay debt.'

Lucia looked horrified.

'Oh no, no. Not that. Duke Wilmslow is a lot of things, but not like that as far as I know. I translate books for him, 'cos I can read and write in many languages.'

'Nay,' Lucia said, her deep brown eyes wide as saucers. 'What language?' she added as if daring Henry to prove himself.

'English, French, Latin, Arabic . . .' Henry smiled. He wanted to say, *Any language in the world, even dead languages, because books* talk *to me . . .*

'How you learn?' Lucia asked.

'It's a long story.'

Lucia looked at Henry and laughed as if she did not believe him.

They had been talking so long and Henry had been so fixed on Lucia that he had not noticed they were now deep in slum territory. With his expensive clothes and cloak, Henry felt as if all eyes were secretly watching him, plotting. His cloak alone would be worth as much as many people around here made in a year or more. Some of the lads Henry had grown up with had killed people for way less.

Henry pulled his cloak back subtly to reveal the dagger sheathed on his waist. Better that people knew he was armed and prepared to fight than try to rob him and make him use it.

Lucia stopped walking. 'Here we are,' she said, taking a key from her pocket and unlocking the door. She gestured for Henry to walk in, but Henry gestured right back at her.

'Ladies first,' he said. Lucia smiled and walked in. As she climbed the stairs Henry watched her strong legs move and felt warm inside.

Even though they were in a run-down tenement block, the room was actually quite nice inside, Henry thought. The walls were decorated with paintings, the bed was a large four-poster that took up most of the room, and thin sheets draped invitingly over each side of the bed, giving it the feel of a private chamber.

Henry felt a touch on his arm. Lucia kissed him and Henry kissed her back.

'Calm, slowly,' Lucia instructed as she pushed him back on to the bed.

Henry tossed in his sleep, Mary's quivering lip and crushed eyes pulling a guilt through him that kept him dreaming. He felt he could wake from it at will, but his guilt wanted to punish him. Mary cried and Henry cried through her, feeling her tears roll down his sleeping face, feeling the lump in her throat and the betrayal in her soul.

Henry's mother looked at Mary and smiled.

She uses the arts the general showed her and manages to
keep alive in the land of these new strangers.
She loves a man; she loves more than one man. She bears
a child, a man child, to one of the strangers.

Henry woke with a start. He looked down, turned his body away from Lucia and pulled on his linen underdrawers, nearly tripping over as he tried to get his foot in. He threw on the rest of his clothes as quickly as possible, sat up and started pulling on his shoes.

'Why you rush?' Lucia asked.

Henry turned to look at her. She was lying on her front, smiling up at him. As Henry remembered last night, he was haunted by what older boys had told him about their first times: how they'd *done it* five times in the same night. Henry had done it once, very quickly, and fallen asleep.

'I must go to the duke,' Henry said.

Lucia got up from the bed and walked towards Henry. He could not look her directly in the eyes. Lucia kissed him delicately on the forehead, and her touch made him feel a little better.

'He not at home. I take you,' she announced.

Henry wanted to ask her how she knew where to take him, how she knew Wilmslow at all. Another one of Graham's sayings came to him: *Don't ask questions if you are not ready for the answer.*

Lucia led Henry to a large, beautiful building on the Strand,

215

and sure enough, parked outside was the duke's carriage. Through the glass door, Henry saw that the duke's guard was asleep inside. He did not want to wake him, but he supposed he had no choice and knocked on the window. The guard bolted up, trying to hide the fact that he had been sleeping.

'What hour do you call this?' he said to Henry through the glass. 'I have been waiting here half the lightmans for you. Wilmslow rode back on his own. He's not in the habit of waiting for his servants. Get in.'

Henry turned to Lucia and waved, even though he wanted so badly to kiss her. 'Adieu.'

'Adieu,' Lucia replied and blew Henry a kiss as he hopped into the carriage.

All Henry could think about was Mary during the ride back to the duke's mansion. He saw the devastated look on her face when he had said those words – *She is just my annoying little cousin* – and guilt weighed on him far greater than his joy at last night's experience. He had to find Mary and apologise as soon as possible.

They arrived at the house and Henry got out of the carriage. One of the duke's servants opened the door and for a moment Henry imagined that this mansion was his home. He shook his head and quickly went to search for Mary. He looked in the kitchen, but she was not there, nor in any of the major halls. She had to be in the stables, the last place Henry wanted to look. Just seeing Mary in the stables, knowing that was where she lived, brought him into a conflict with himself that was far too much to bear.

The stables were empty but Camilla was outside milking a cow. 'Where's Mary?' Henry asked, instantly annoyed at himself for not even saying hello first.

Camilla looked up from her task, the contempt in her eyes making Henry feel smaller than he'd thought possible. 'Gone,' she said, her lip curling upwards in disgust. 'Thanks to you.'

'What do you mean, gone?'

'I mean *gone*, Henry. Ain't you supposed to be the clever one? I'm sure you are familiar with the word.'

Henry could not believe how Camilla was talking to him. Seeing her serve him dinner and clean up after him so meekly and obediently, he'd almost begun to think she was his servant too. But the stinging tone of her words reminded him she certainly was not.

'Gone where?'

'Gone who knows where. Someone hurt her. Someone she has been to hell and back with, someone she has stood by and loved since as long as she can remember, fobbed her off like a stranger, just because he got a little taste of the high life and had a doxy he wanted to impress. Hurt like that makes a person do silly things, Henry. Who knows where she has run away to? Anywhere to get away from you, I suppose.'

There was so much love in the way that Camilla spoke, despite her harsh words, it was worse than if she'd just cussed him outright.

'Did you give her my message, all those weeks ago?' Henry demanded. 'I waited for her at midnight, but she never came.'

'Waited there every darkmans like you promised, did you . . . ?' Camilla replied. Henry felt ashamed. He'd given up after only one try, and Camilla knew it. 'Why would I fill her head with that foolishness?' Camilla replied.

'You had no right to make that decision,' Henry said. 'I was going to run away, take her with me, but now she has run off anyway. At least with my help, she'd have had a better chance of getting by.'

Camilla scoffed. 'You are even more full of yourself than I thought if you think that little woman needs *you* to get by. And don't try to pin your sins on me.'

Henry tried to think of a comeback, for a way to defend himself and his actions, but all he felt was shame.

Henry searched the house for Wilmslow until there was only one place left that he could be: the library. As Henry arrived at the door, he thought about turning back and leaving the matter alone, but each time he went to turn, his feet would not carry him away.

Each time he lifted his hand to knock on the library door, a weak feeling in his stomach forced his hand back down again.

Finally, his hand discovered its own courage and knocked.

'Enter,' the duke shouted through the door. Henry entered

the room to find the duke sitting at his desk, working on some documents.

This was the first time Henry had been in the library since the robbery. He wondered why the duke had never brought him back in here. The books had always been brought to Henry and he'd always had to work in his own room or in the underground club. He had never been allowed to work in the most logical place: the library. Of course, Henry quickly realised, this was the duke's own sacred space. This was his church. And this was where he came to write his diaries.

'To what do I owe this visit, Henry?' the duke said, without looking up from his work.

'Sir, I am sorry. I have done something bad, but I promise I can fix it.'

The duke's face contorted, adding several extra wrinkles to his forehead.

'What have you done?'

'Well, after you left me yesterday, I saw Mary at the theatre. I was horrible to her, acted like I barely knew her, 'cos . . . 'cos I wanted to impress Lucia. Now Mary has run away 'cos she is hurt, but I promise if you let me, I'll go find her and apologise and bring her back. Please sir, please.'

'*Because*,' the duke said without emotion.

'What? I mean, pardon, sir?'

'It's *because*, not '*cos*. I thought you were learning to speak properly.'

'Sorry, sir, but please can I go and find Mary?'

'Henry?' The duke asked his name as a question, still scribbling in his notebook as he spoke.

'Yes, sir.'

'What do you think would happen if every clever man abandoned his work and threw his life to the wind each time a silly little girl got her feelings hurt?'

'Pardon, sir?'

The duke put his pen down and looked to the wall in front of him.

'Mary is a spoiled little girl. She has run away from the lap of luxury, to Lord knows what, all because you said something she did not like. Oh, imagine if we could all just do as we liked every time somebody said something that offended us?'

'But, sir—'

'But nothing,' the duke interrupted. 'So the base little wench wants to run back where she belongs.' The duke finally turned away from his desk to look at Henry. 'Let her go. She was of no real use to me anyway. She can't cook, she is too young for my bed and her presence here no longer serves to discipline you – you, who are of some value – because you have learned that working with me is in your interests too. Leave her to starve; ignore her as you rightly did yesterday. You have the chance to become a better class of man than that mouthy little wench ever can. Don't throw that away for her.'

Henry could not help but flinch at the duke's unkind words. 'But, sir, by your gracious patience, she's my friend and I'd like to go and find her.'

The duke closed his workbooks slowly before responding. 'And I want the moon on a stick, so what?'

'Please, sir. I just want to make sure she is safe.'

'If harm should come to her, she only has herself to blame. She chose to run away. Now be gone and let me get back to my work, boy.'

Henry flinched again at the word 'boy'. Older men used it as if they had not been children themselves just a few moons ago – as if being a boy was some kind of a curse.

'Why are you so heartless?' Henry said.

The duke gripped the arms of his chair with both hands as if it was all he could do to restrain himself. 'Heartless? Heartless?' the duke repeated. 'You ungrateful little swine. Have you forgotten why you are even alive, why you are not still in that dungeon? Have you forgotten who pays for the clothes on your back, the food in your stomach and the roof over your head?'

'I do plenty for you in return! And anyway, I did not ask for all this.' Henry knew he was fighting a losing battle, but he had lost control. He wasn't going to apologise.

'You took it though, didn't you? You tried to resist for about five minutes, but one little taste of the high life and . . .' The Duke paused. 'Just look at you.'

Henry knew that he looked ridiculous, standing here in one of the best libraries in the kingdom, dressed in clothes that cost more than the house he had grown up in, the little Moor from Devil's Gap.

'I did what I had to do to survive.' Henry wished he had come up with something cleverer to say, but the duke let go of the chair arms and seemed to relax slightly.

'Tell yourself whatever it pleases you to tell, Henry. You took it and you loved it, and now you feel guilty because your little lovebird, sister, cousin, thing – whatever the hell she is – has thrown a tantrum.'

'Don't call her a thing,' Henry said, unable to suppress the rage in his tone.

The duke jumped out of his seat, rage visibly pulsing through a vein in his forehead. 'Are you telling me what to do in my own home, boy?' the duke whispered, making his anger all the more scary.

'Look, sir, I just want to go and find Mary. I want to check in on my family. I have served you well, haven't I? I will be back by nightfall, I promise. You can even send your guard to watch over me.' Henry had not meant to mention his family, but he was intending to go and check in on Joan and Matthew too.

The duke took a step closer to Henry and smiled. 'Family. Help. Promise.' The duke's face twisted with each word. 'All these meaningless words together. Those people are not your family. The only way you can help me is by doing the work that has kept you alive, and the promises of a half-Moorish thief are less than worthless to me.'

'They are my family. You've no idea what we been through together.'

The duke exploded with a loud, exaggerated laugh. He stepped even closer to Henry.

Henry did not step back. The duke carried on laughing, right in Henry's face now.

'What?' Henry asked. 'What so amuses you?'

The duke looked Henry straight in the eyes, their faces so close that Henry could feel the duke's breath as he spoke. 'It's funny that you really believe these people love you. Bless you, you naïve little child. Yes, I want you for what you can do for me, but at least I am honest with you about my motivations. Unlike that witch Joan, who wants you for all the same selfish reasons I do, but because she can't do for you what I can, she pretends to love you. And you being the gullible child you still are, you actually believe her.' The duke was still laughing, making his words seem crueller to Henry. 'Do you really think she would have taken in an abandoned tawny Blackamoor if you were not so gifted? You have seen countless other homeless children in this city and she has not taken them in. What makes you so special, if not your gift?'

Henry went to speak but no words would come. *No*, he thought. *Joan loves me. She's sacrificed so much for me through the years. Mary definitely loves me, Matthew too, in his own way, but* . . . The rage boiled inside Henry as the spite of the duke's words really sank in.

'Just because your family died, it does not mean you have to be such a bitter and horrible—'

Clap!

The duke's slap stopped Henry in mid-sentence, the sheer force of it telling Henry that fighting back would be useless – though striking a duke would be a death sentence anyway. Henry stumbled backwards, clutching his stinging face.

'I wanted to protect you from the real truth, you ungrateful little swine, but seeing as you have the audacity to talk about my family, I will bother no more. You are an idiot if you believe that these people love you – a genius, but an idiot. If they love you so much, how come they set you up to get caught robbing my house, knowing how I'd punish you? Knowing that if you did not perform for me I'd probably have you hanged? Or are you so stupid that you still think it was just a coincidence that I came home so soon that night?'

The words slapped Henry harder than the duke himself had. Rage churned his guts and he bit his lip so hard he tasted blood. He clenched his fists, digging his fingers into his palms. The realisations came crashing down on him.

Of course Agnes was the connection for the robbery, that's why she let me get away without punishment. And Matthew . . . he was so angry about Mary following us to the duke's house . . . and he pretended to be so concerned with her safety, wanting her to stay with him during the robbery. He must have been involved too.

It was now clear why Matthew had made peace with him so easily, unlike his usual stubborn self. Henry could not believe he had been so naïve.

That's why the duke knew my name, and about Joan and Agnes from the very beginning.

The duke was not finished though; he had the smug face of a card-game player holding a winning hand. He watched Henry's pain, smiling the way people smiled watching dogs and bears tear each other to pieces, taking pleasure in the sight of blood.

Henry pictured Matthew next to him in the bear pit, beaming as if he were excited about catching another coney together, when really he knew that he was setting his best friend up for a foist that could lead to his death. *Treacherous knave.*

Henry remembered Matthew throwing the bread on the floor and suddenly it hit him. *Maybe they'd been planning to set me up for a while. Only someone certain that they had money coming in would ever throw away bread, surely? How could Matthew, the worst thief among us, ever be so confident?* Either way, it was clear that while Henry could be sacrificed, Mary could not. As usual *they* protected their own, and even in the closest thing Henry had known to a family, he was still a worthless outsider.

The sound of the duke's voice broke Henry's thoughts.

'And if Joan loves you so much, then why has she not told you that your mother is alive and well and that she wrote asking after you?'

The duke had somehow pitched his voice exactly like a dagger, which stabbed and twisted inside Henry's stomach. Henry struggled to process the words while the duke continued turning the blade.

'I am sure you have seen that guilty look in Joan's eyes and wondered what it was. Well, now you know. Damn, Mary probably even knows too.'

Henry was pierced by a stabbing headache, his vision suddenly blurry. He felt a heat inside his body that he had never known before as anger mixed with betrayal and grief smashed through him all at once. It took all his strength to just hold himself up.

'But *you* knew my mum was alive too. You did not say anything either . . .'

The duke scoffed. 'People need such simplistic fairy tales to survive this world. You seemed so content lying to yourself about your adopted family, I did not want to ruin the illusion for you. But then you decided to talk about *my* family, boy.'

Henry remembered the duke's diary and how he had felt reading it; that the man really loved his wife and children. Henry knew he'd made a mistake but there was no turning back now. His head was spinning with the revelation that his mother was alive and well and Joan, of all people, had known it.

The duke put his hand on Henry's shoulder. 'Look, Henry, I am willing to forgive you for talking about my family as long as you never make that mistake again. You and I will never be family. But I thought we had got to an understanding before this latest little outburst.'

Henry looked around at the magnificent library and thought about all the new things the duke had introduced to him – the food, the clothes, the expensive seats at the theatre, his first bed, his first hot bath, Spanish leather shoes, Lucia.

Perhaps the duke was right. They had developed a kind of understanding.

But my mother is alive. Surely that changes everything?

'Get some sleep and we'll start again tomorrow, eh?' the duke said, removing his hand from Henry's shoulder.

Henry could not speak, so he just smiled through pursed lips, nodded and turned to go to his room.

But the curse under which the general was placed all those moons ago – back before the first of the wars in the old kingdom – will not leave her. Eshu is upon her family.

Elegba, the trickster God, drinks well.

16

Henry's mother appeared as Graham, their faces somehow merged. He saw Mary running. His mother and Graham both judged him through one pair of eyes and Graham's voice spoke through his mother's lips.

'Sometimes in life a man must make his own mistakes.'

Henry jumped out of bed and immediately got dressed. He headed for the door almost without a thought, but something pulled him back: he needed to prepare for the possibility he'd be running away forever. There was no telling what would happen once he jumped out of that window.

He picked up a cloth bag, loaded it with a few of the books he was currently working on for the duke, some writing paper, quills and ink, then tiptoed out of his room and along the corridor, up one floor to the washing place. The door creaked open as he pushed it and Henry shook, fighting to control his nerves. He walked up to the bathtub and lifted with all his might, the floorboards groaning horrendously under the weight of the bath. Henry pulled harder and harder. Somehow, the bath seemed to be heavier without any water in it. Finally he got it up high enough to slip his toe under the hollow foot and kick the golden bird away.

As the bird scuttled across the floor, Henry tried to let the bath down as gently as he could, the floorboards growling in protest. He removed the bird from its pouch and held it up to the candlelight. It really was just as beautiful as he had remembered. *How could human hands make things this pretty?* Henry returned the bird to the pouch and slipped it into his breeches.

Carrying his shoes in his hands, he tiptoed through the house, reaching the kitchen window and opening it slowly, one small crack at a time. With each push, a sharp creaking sound echoed around the kitchen, which, together with the wind gusting in from outside, rattled the hanging pots. After each movement, he listened out for footsteps and then pushed the window open a little more. Henry just wanted to yank it open and be done with it but that would certainly wake someone up. Nervous sweat started to tickle his forehead.

The voices of doubt grew louder with each bead of sweat that ran down his face, until finally the window was open wide enough. His heart racing, Henry pulled on his shoes and climbed through. He lowered himself towards the ground by holding on to the window ledge with his fingertips. He looked down over his right shoulder, remembering the last time he had dropped from this window, the feeling of Mary's hand slipping away from his, the sight of her body dangling in the air and the stone-cold look on the guard's face.

He closed his eyes and tried to relax his muscles – a lifetime of climbing, running and being chased had taught him that falls hurt much more when you tense up – and let go of the window ledge.

Henry managed to land much more skilfully than last time, but still needed a moment to let the stinging pain shooting through his ankles and knees subside. He adjusted the cloth bag on his back, took one last look up at the duke's mansion and then started to march.

The torches on the corners of each street made London look pretty in the night-time, the flames flickering in the breeze making the city feel like the warm inside of someone's home. In this semi-darkness Henry could not see the filth that lined the streets, only the faint orange glow on the sides of buildings. He passed several inns and heard the merry songs coming from inside – the sounds of the lute accompanied by the out-of-tune sing-along of London's pub-goers. As he passed through the French Quarter, he remembered the game he and Mary played with his gift and the shop signs. Henry walked a little faster.

Night-time London was even stranger than daytime London; the smell of desserts, coffee and tobacco overpowered the daytime stink, the happy songs from the pubs and the alluring lights masked the danger of the city at this hour. The watch were patrolling as always, but even their presence would not be enough to stop people getting robbed on their way home from the alehouse. Many of those happy drinking songs would still descend into knife fights and some poor lady of the night was still destined to end up in a ditch somewhere.

Night-time London and everyone in it was a sham, a façade luring you in with promises of a hot meal and sweet words – when really all she wanted to do was use you. Fake – just like Joan and Mary and Matthew. Agnes and Wilmslow were the real London: cruel and brutal. London didn't lie to you unless you let it, and neither could people unless you let them, Henry decided.

Henry arrived at the apothecary and paced up and down outside the door, running through his planned conversation. He imagined how he would curse Joan out, telling her what a hypocrite and a user she was.

He steadied himself and knocked on the door once, twice and then again and again . . . until the speed of the thumps created an ill-timed beat. He heard neighbours groan in their beds, a voice shouting, 'Shut up!' but he just could not stop his hand.

Joan arrived at the door in her nightgown, dagger in hand. It seemed to take her a moment to adjust her vision.

'Henry?' she said. Joan took another look, moving her head as if that would improve her sight. 'Henry,' she said again, this time a statement, not a question.

Henry's anger turned to something strange as he stood there. Joan looked as if she had aged ten years since last summer, her body a frail shadow of the woman he remembered. Too weak to properly inspire anger.

Joan leaned in to hug him and Henry hugged her back half-heartedly. Just a second ago he had sworn to himself that he would give Joan a piece of his mind, but now he felt nervous and unsure. Could this withered old woman really be responsible for the pain he was feeling?

Henry walked down the stairs and Joan followed after him, moving so slowly it made Henry's natural speed feel like a cruel taunt.

Joan went to sit at her desk but then changed her mind. 'We'll go through to the back room. You must have missed it.' Henry just followed her, not saying a word.

The back room was just as he remembered it. He looked at all those books, taking them in properly for the first time; he had basically given Joan a small library. If she chose to sell them, these books would be worth a fortune.

Who knows – maybe she has been making extra copies of my translations and secretly selling them all these years? Henry could not tell whether he should feel betrayed or proud, looking at the shelves. *Am I a genius or an idiot?*

'You must be hungry. Let me fix you something to eat,' Joan said. 'I don't have much, as usual, but I'm sure I can rustle up something.'

'I'm fine,' Henry replied.

'So, talk to me. How are you? I've missed you like bedlam. Matthew told me what happened and I tried to come and find you, I offered the duke all the money I have, potions that men crave and anything else I could think of to get you both back, but he was having none of it.' Joan was talking very fast. She seemed a little stronger now Henry could see the light in her eyes properly. There was that cleverness that Henry remembered, even though it was clear her sight was fading. 'How did you get away?' Joan continued. 'I told you about that stealing now, didn't I? And look at you, with your fancy caster and Spanish leather stampers.' The grey of Joan's hair had somehow darkened, the locks were spindly and thin like a cheap actor's wig; the wrinkles of her skin were as deep as the frills in a ruff.

Henry stared at his hands and played with his palms. He wanted to tell Joan all about the last few months and everything he had been through; he wanted to tell her how much he'd missed her. But he could not do that until he knew. Henry swallowed.

'Is it true?' he said.

'Is what true?' Joan replied.

'You know what.'

'No, I don't, Henry. What's the matter?' Joan looked genuinely worried and Henry thought about leaving it. *Is it really fair to break this old woman's heart? But she knows about your mother. She's been lying to you, Henry.*

'Is it true that my mum has been writing to you, asking about me, and you did not say anything?' There was no turning back now.

The blood drained from Joan's face instantly, confirming the truth. Henry's mind swirled with confusion and fury even though he'd known it must be true, because how else would the duke have known? He had hoped there was a way out, some kind of mix-up perhaps – but the stunned look on Joan's face was all the admission of guilt he needed. Henry gazed around the room at all the books he had translated and saw nothing but volumes of lies – pages and pages of testament to Joan's betrayal.

'I can explain,' Joan pleaded, an innocent tone in her voice that made Henry's ears burn. *What a deceitful witch. Look at her, pretending butter would not melt.*

'What is there to explain?' Henry shouted. 'You knew, you knew, you knew!' His tone changed from accusation to statement and back again as he repeated the phrase. 'You knew that my mother is alive and you did not tell me. What in God's name is there to explain?'

'Henry, I was just trying to protect you.'

'Protect me?' Henry could feel the rage twisting his face, shaking his hands. He looked around again at the books in the room, taunting him. Henry jumped up, tipped over a shelf and started ripping out pages.

'Henry, stop! What are you doing?' Joan pleaded.

Henry just carried on ripping. Joan tried to hold him back but he easily moved around her and carried on destroying the books. The horror on Joan's face gave him nothing but satisfaction, but a part of him also flinched at each ripped page. It felt like sacrilege to destroy any book, let alone ruin years of his own work.

A shot of Joan's *chi* energy hit him in the hand, knocking a book away. He fought against it as hard as he could, but her energy was just too strong. It pushed him up against the wall, squashing his body like a fat man leaning on him. Henry pushed and pushed, but it was no use. That was the thing about *chi* energy – the harder you struggled against it, the stronger it got. He gave up struggling and started crying with rage instead.

'Why?' he asked, piercing Joan with his tear-filled eyes.

Joan reached out a hand to the desk to steady herself, clearly drained from using her magic.

'You look old,' Henry said, deliberately spiteful, 'but at least it makes you appear more like the witch that you are.'

Joan walked out of the room. Henry could not believe that she had just left without saying a word. He heard her rummaging through a drawer, mumbling a word he didn't understand, and then she hobbled back into the room.

'Here is your mother's letter,' Joan said, handing it to Henry.

'My mother's letter?' Henry asked, holding it as if it were the golden bird.

'Yes, Henry.'

Henry paced with the letter in his hand. Its paper was a little finer and lighter than the usual stuff. He looked from Joan to the letter and back. It had all been just talk until now; having his mother's letter had upped the stakes more than Henry was prepared for.

Henry unfolded the letter, looked at the page and read the words aloud. '*How is the boy?*' Henry was confused. '*How is the boy?*' he said again, trying to make sense of it. 'That's all it says.

How do you even know it's from my mother?'

'I know her handwriting a mile away, and that's what she would say.'

'*How is the boy?*' Henry said again. 'She talks as if I were some random stranger, not her child.'

'It's not that, Henry. Your mother does love you, it's just the curse—'

'The curse?' Henry cut in, throwing the letter to the floor. 'Witch crap again. How can I believe anything you say now? For all I know, you kidnapped me from my mum so you could use me for all this.' Henry gestured to the shelves.

'You really believe I would do that, Henry?'

Henry raised his voice just below a shout. 'I don't know what you would do!' He turned his back to Joan, thinking for a moment. 'The duke said you knew where she was?'

'Ay, back in Venice.'

'How do you know?' Henry demanded.

'I asked the messenger where the letter had come from. Look, he—'

Henry whipped round and cut Joan a sharp look that told her to be quiet. He could only stand there, repeating the phrase over and over to himself. *How is the boy? How is the boy?* His mind drifted from his mother to the duke and then to how he had ended up in the duke's dungeon.

'Did you know Matthew and Agnes set me up? Like a proper little apple-squire,' Henry said with a sly laugh, reflecting on the irony of himself – a master thief – being so easily tricked.

'You were probably in on it too, weren't you, now that I had served my purpose.' Henry gestured to the books again. 'How many shells did Wilmslow pay you lot?'

'I'm sure Matthew would not do that. But . . . well . . . Agnes is Agnes.'

'Bunch of knaves and Turks, the lot of you,' Henry said. He looked at the letter discarded on the floor, his rage weakening and giving way to pain. He looked at Joan's face, at her pointed nose and her angry lips. How had he not seen the deceit plastered all over it before now?

Exhausted, Henry looked again at Joan and around at the carnage he had created. He did not feel satisfied, but instead, terrified, and he could not explain why. He picked up his mother's letter from the floor and ran.

'Henry, I was only trying to protect you,' Joan called after him as he leaped up the stairs.

'Henry, please . . .' Joan's voice faded into the background as Henry opened the door and ran out on to the street. He turned around and looked up at the place he had called home all of these years and he thought about going to confront Matthew. But even with this amount of rage he still did not want to have to confront Agnes too. Instead, Henry ran. He did not think about where his feet were taking him. A constable shouted for him to stop, but Henry knew the man could not catch him. He noticed the few passers-by crossing the street to get away from the crazy man sprinting around at night.

Henry only stopped when he collapsed in a pile outside

Graham's front door, sobbing.

The morning sun woke Henry up a moment before he heard Graham's voice.

'What possessed you to couch your hogshead outside, lad? You could have got bitten by a rat or killed by nightmen or anything.' His tone seemed hurt. Graham ushered Henry inside, examining his body so keenly that Henry wondered if he was actually looking for evidence of rat bites.

'It was darkmans and I didn't want to wake you,' Henry said, taking a seat by the fire. He covered himself in the blanket Graham handed him, though in truth he was not that cold. He had slept outside before, and that was without a duke's cloak to keep him warm.

'So, what brings you to visit us common folk anyway? I thought you was a noble now? I see you've come suitably trimmed.' Graham laughed, gesturing at Henry's clothes.

Henry smiled, trying to hide his discomfort while imagining how out of place he must look to Graham's eyes. His ruff probably cost more than every item of clothing Graham owned.

Graham's workshop – which had once seemed so large in comparison to Henry's tenement home – now seemed tiny in comparison to the duke's kitchen, let alone the mansion's halls.

Graham poured a beer for both of them. 'Well, it seems some of those dreams of yours came true. Good job you did not listen

241

to me and end up stuck here.' The bitterness and intimidation in Graham's voice hurt Henry, but it was his own fault. He should not have come here looking like this.

'So what happened, lad?' Graham asked more seriously.

'Well, me and Mary got caught stealing from—'

'I know that part,' Graham cut in. 'The streets do talk, you know.'

Henry looked away to avoid the *I told you so* gaze that was surely written in the old man's eyes.

'Well, at first the duke locked me in a cell, battered me and half-starved me to death . . .' Henry recounted the whole story – everything that had happened since the night of the robbery – the bath, the food, Lucia, his betrayal of Mary. All apart from the details of his gift. For some reason, he had never told Graham and he could not work out why. Now would have been the time to tell him, but it just seemed too much like more showing off. So he pretended he just did straightforward translations for the duke and his friends.

As Henry spoke, Graham took some kippers from a bag, skewered them and placed them over the fire, the sweet smell of roasted fish filling the air. 'I hope these are acceptable to one's refined palette?' Graham joked as he sat down.

Henry nodded, distracted by his continuing story. 'I got to live in the house. I even had my own room, with a proper bed and everything. Me and the duke, well, we never became friends, but we got along adequately in the end.'

'You got along *adequately*, did ya?'

Henry smiled. 'Ay, well, if you are around noble folk long enough, stuff kind of rubs off.'

'I'm just playing with you, lad.' Graham smiled a wide, warm smile, the skin around the top of his cheekbones and his eyes bunching together. It gave his old face such a baby-like quality that Henry could imagine what he'd looked like as a child. Henry sank further into the chair, his nervousness drifting away.

For a long while Graham just stared at Henry without saying anything. Finally, he spoke. 'I am sure you feel betrayed right now, lad, and that's understandable. If Matthew really did cozen you, that's proper rascally even by your thief code, I'm sure. I don't know Joan that well, but enough to believe she was only trying to protect you.'

'Not you as well, Graham. That's the same tilly-vally she said.'

'Ever thought that she might be right? You know I like you a lot, lad, so don't take this the wrong way, but it seems to me like you are naïve about how the world works – and how people work. A little spoiled, even, which is strange for someone who grew up as tough as you.' Graham tilted his head knowingly at Henry. 'Maybe you was a high-born in a past life.' Graham looked at Henry's shoes and they both laughed. Henry thought about what Joan had said about his mother probably being high-born. *Me, high-born? No way.*

'I doubt it,' Henry replied.

'Let's think about it. You got caught milling a ken. You was lucky enough not just to escape death or Newgate, but to land in the lap of luxury working for a rich and powerful duke – not scrubbing floors or cleaning out the latrines, but doing something you love.' Graham's tone was almost mocking, making Henry's gripes seem so trivial, the words crushing him with their truth.

'So the duke starved you and beat you a bit? Boohoo. Which poor person anywhere has not nearly died from hunger during a bad harvest or not been battered or stocked or whipped by a vicious lord?' Graham looked at Henry as if it was really a question. 'And how many of us get to eat rabbit pie and wear a duke's clothes at the end of it? And you've run away because your equally spoiled cousin disappeared in a tantrum because you were not nice to her?' Graham scoffed. 'If every man threw his life to the wind each time a little girl ran away from home, the world would collapse, lad.'

Henry could not believe how much Graham sounded like the duke and the doctors. Maybe all old men thought the same way, regardless of rank.

'I get that you are upset about Joan and your mum,' Graham continued. 'But how is running away and risking your safety and your life going to change that? You want my advice? Go back to the duke now, apologise and beg him to have you back. You've no idea what it's like to be a masterless man out in this world, foolish boy.'

Henry knew Graham was right, but he remembered something the old man had said to him once.

'But a man must live to make his own mistakes; he cannot live the life of another.'

Graham smiled. 'You're too bloody quick-mettled for your own good, you know that, lad?' He ruffled Henry's hair and got up to turn over the kippers. 'So what are you going to do then?'

'I am going to go to Venice to look for my mother.'

'Oh sweet Lord Jesus.' Graham immediately panicked for taking the Lord's name in vain and crossed himself, which made Henry smile. 'You are even more crazy than I thought. Have you ever been on the high seas, lad? Of course you have not. Well, I have.'

Graham picked up his pipe and began stuffing it methodically with tobacco. To Henry, Graham had always had the grand, graceful movements of an actor, even in doing small things such as this. Graham started smoking, taking a few deep breaths – as if he needed the hit before he could further deal with Henry.

Finally Graham spoke through the tobacco smoke, the pipe giving him the aura of a gentleman. 'If you think life is tough in Devil's Gap, try to imagine if Devil's Gap was floating on a storm, with only the worst people in the slum on board. No rich people to steal from or sell to – and loads of other Devil's Gaps floating around it, filled with pirates ready to climb aboard, kill everyone and take what little you have. That's life on the high seas.'

To Henry this sounded exciting, but he did not want to be cocky and tell Graham that. 'But you survived it, right? And it got you here, away from Spain, to a better life. You said so yourself.'

Graham laughed at Henry again. 'You really are too bloody smart.' Graham took the kippers off the fire and handed Henry a few on a small wooden slab. 'Sorry – no fine china around here, good sir,' Graham said with a bow.

'Thanks,' Henry said, biting into a hot kipper and feeling its warmth hit his stomach before he had even swallowed.

'So how do you plan to pay for this trip and what will you do when you get there?'

Henry put the slab down, reached into his breeches and pulled out the golden bird. Graham's face dropped with amazement as he took in the beauty of it. 'I was hoping you could help me get some shells for this,' Henry said.

Graham chewed his kipper, looking from Henry to the bird and back again a few times. 'It's beautiful,' he said. 'And you know I'd love to help you, but I can't risk my freedom, lad, nor should you. Even though you got wool between your ears, I'll say it: the duke will be looking for you and for his little bird . . . and he may not be so forgiving this time.

'Look, lad, when I was your age, I was just as hard-headed, so don't think I don't understand, but it cost me dearly . . .' Graham trailed off.

'I didn't want to come to you,' Henry said, 'but I know you know people, and if you don't help me I'll have to go to the Southside and the risk of getting caught is even greater.'

'Don't you dare try to force that on to me, lad!' Graham raised his voice. 'I told you not to do any of this; it ain't my responsibility or fault to fix your foolishness.'

Henry went silent. They both just stared at each other.

'I am going to Venice,' Henry repeated with conviction. 'I have to at least look for my mother, or I'll just live the rest of my life wondering what if.'

From the change in Graham's expression, Henry saw he had finally won the argument. 'Fair enough, lad, fair enough,' Graham replied, his tone more resigned than respectful. He got up and ruffled Henry's hair again before walking across the room to a drawer. 'If you are gonna travel on the seas, I am sure you will need this.' He handed Henry a vial full of liquid. 'Best cure for sea sickness ever. Believe you me, you will need it. But whatever you do, do *not*' – Graham said the word 'not' so hard it almost sounded like a drumbeat – 'drink wine before or after you take it. You'll crap your guts out if you do. And here are a few shells towards the venture.' Graham dropped a few coins into Henry's hand. 'It's not enough to buy you passage, but it's a start.'

Henry wanted to say no thank you, but he was in no position to reject the old man's money. Who knew how long it would take him to sell the bird?

Henry stood up intending to give Graham a firm, manly handshake, but he found himself hugging the old man instead.

'Thank you,' Henry said, fighting the lump forming in his throat.

'No trouble, lad, no trouble.' They stepped back from the hug and Henry saw Graham's eyes were ringed red. He told himself it was just from decades of working the furnace.

Everything she tries: potion, prayer, meditation, spell.

Still she cannot shake the voice of the curse.

Demons come in the night to devour her man child;

she fights them away, just.

The walk from the steel yard to the Southside was right across town. Henry's paranoia made the distance seem even further than usual. His heart jumped every time someone looked at him, imagining they were about to apprehend him and collect whatever prize money or favour the duke had certainly offered as reward for his capture.

He took the back alleys instead of going straight up Thames Street, battling the urge to run. Because no one in London ever ran, unless they were running for their lives.

Henry reflected on Graham's advice. If Henry went back to the duke now he probably *would* be forgiven, but for how long? What would happen when Wilmslow changed his mind or decided that Henry had served his purpose?

Mary crept into his thoughts and he pushed her away. Joan's pleading face replaced Mary's and he prickled with anger. Matthew's bloody nose appeared to him and Henry smiled at the image.

He reached the busiest part of the Southside and crouched among a pile of rubbish in a small corner of an alleyway. He could see everything from here – the Globe, the bear-baiting arena, the alehouses. Thieves were up and down here all day, making deals and plotting future schemes. It was only a matter of time before one of the chief priggers Henry knew passed by, but for now, he would just have to hold his nerve and wait. There was a sweaty heat in the air, even though the sun was hidden behind a wall of light-grey clouds, and Henry's armpits were wet from the walk. He pulled up the sleeve of his cloak and wiped his brow with the cuff of his shirt. *These bloody noble clothes are no good in summer*, he thought.

As he crouched there, most of the passing people did not give Henry a second glance. But each time someone did notice him, he saw the strange look in their eyes as they processed his brown skin and then his fine clothes, no doubt wondering why he was hidden among rubbish. Henry knew he was making himself a target.

A group of young boys walked past for the third time, all staring Henry dead in the face. He knew their look well – he had given it himself, many times before. They were envious of his clothes and all they signalled; they were thinking about robbing him but frightened of the consequences; they were looking for signs of weakness and fear.

Henry stared back, putting menace behind his look to let them know that he was not the one to try it with. The boys walked off.

A group of finely clothed women were talking to some men as they passed by. Among them Henry was shocked to recognise Lucia. She was talking to a man and it was clear from her body language that they knew each other well. Henry remembered that flutter of the eyelids and her inviting smile, and he was annoyed at himself for feeling a pinch of jealousy. He contemplated walking off. There was no telling if the duke had offered Lucia money to help capture Henry, but the Southside was the only place he had a chance in hell of selling this bird quickly and Lucia was only a girl – it was not as if she could catch Henry by herself. Before Henry could decide what to do, Lucia kissed the man on the cheek and started to walk in Henry's direction. He stood up as she got closer and brushed down his cloak, trying to take her attention away from the rubbish.

'Henry?'

'Ay,' Henry replied.

Lucia made some small talk and Henry responded vaguely, trying to gauge what she might know. As she spoke, he noticed new things about her, things that he had not taken in fully the first time: the small brown beauty spot on the far reach of her right cheek that looked like it was trying to tickle her ear; the way her cheekbones and chin came together in smooth, perfectly formed lines, like the image of a person in a painting. He was convinced she did not know yet; she seemed relaxed and calm.

'Come,' Lucia said as she kissed his neck and grabbed his hand. Henry knew it was stupid to follow her, that really he should concentrate on getting rid of the bird, but her perfumed smell was intoxicating and her kiss more delicate than anything Henry had ever felt. She had also just walked away from another man to come over to him, so she must really like him . . . *If I am going to leave London forever, might as well spend my last moments with her.*

The inside of Lucia's apartment did not seem as impressive as it first had to Henry. It was actually just a typical slum tenement with a few wall hangings to make it look exotic and inviting. The ceiling was stained black where the smoke from a neighbour's chimney had seeped through the thin walls, and beneath the drapes Henry could see holes and dents in the walls themselves. The floor was dirty and cracked, the rushes and herbs scattered all over it barely covering its flaws.

Lucia started kissing his neck . . .

As soon as they finished Henry was angry that he'd been so easily distracted, feeling drained but happy. A Shakespeare sonnet he'd never understood before suddenly made sense to him.

> *Th' expense of spirit in a waste of shame*
> *Is lust in action; and till action, lust*
> *Is perjured, murd'rous, bloody, full of blame,*
> *Savage, extreme, rude, cruel, not to trust,*
> *Enjoyed no sooner but despisèd straight,*
> *Past reason hunted; and, no sooner had*
> *Past reason hated as a swallowed bait*
> *On purpose laid to make the taker mad;*

Mad in pursuit and in possession so,
Had, having, and in quest to have, extreme;
A bliss in proof and proved, a very woe;
Before, a joy proposed; behind, a dream.
All this the world well knows; yet none knows well
To shun the heaven that leads men to this hell.

Henry hopped out of the bed, picked up his breeches and went to throw them back on. The conk of a sound on the floorboards took his eyes across the room, following the sound. The velvet pouch hit the floor and the golden bird rolled out of it, skitting along and stopping by Lucia's side of the bed. She got up to see what it was.

'What is this? Lucia asked, picking the golden bird up from the floor. She had the same look as Graham when he'd first seen the bird – as if she could not process its beauty and was also trying to calculate just how much it would be worth.

Henry snatched the bird from Lucia. 'It's nothing,' he snapped. Lucia held her hands up as if to say, *All right, sorry I asked*, and Henry felt bad for being harsh. He knew he had made a mistake by getting distracted from his plan. He went to leave.

'Why you go so fast?' she asked.

He thought back to their first conversation as they walked along the river and the things Lucia had revealed to him about her own life.

Henry decided to tell her the truth.

255

'My mother is definitely back in Venice. I am going to sail there and find her. Once I sell this golden bird, I am off,' Henry said, tapping his pocket.

'How you know?' Lucia asked.

'The duke and my aunt Joan both knew and they lied to me.'

'Oh,' Lucia said. Henry pulled his cloak around him; he was ready to kiss Lucia goodbye and leave.

'I can sell for you?' Lucia said.

Henry thought about waiting on the Southside alone and all the dangers that brought, the duke's spies must be looking for him by now, not to mention that a chief prigger could easily rob him. Maybe he should give it to her . . . But then he thought about how Lucia had looked at the bird like it was an object of magic, the way even now her eyes seemed to flick to his pocket every few seconds. She too could sell it and disappear forever, or she could give it back to the duke and collect a big reward, and of course, she might just as easily get robbed.

'This very rare. You sell to an Englishman, you get –' Lucia searched for the word – 'problems. Italians take it, no problems and no questions.' She walked over to her dressing table and sat down with her back to Henry.

Henry knew Lucia was right. An object that valuable and rare was bound to arouse suspicion among English priggers, worried they'd not be able to sell it on or be caught because it was so distinctive. Whereas a foreign prigger would just take it and sell it on for even more money somewhere else. Henry did not trust Lucia – he hardly knew her after all – but what real choice did he have? *Maybe her being there on the Southside was God's good fortune finally shining down on me*, Henry thought.

He looked at Lucia in the mirror of her dressing table as she brushed her hair. 'I can come with you and sell it to the Italians myself. I'll pay you a cut?' Henry suggested.

'You don't trust?' Lucia replied, slowly applying red dye to her lips and light blue powder to her eyelids. She got up from her dressing table and looked through him with her big brown eyes. She stepped in, grabbed his hand and kissed him once. Henry closed his eyes, tasting her kiss, opening them again and feeling lost in the fullness of her red lips. He pulled his hand back from hers and tried to regain some composure.

'No, it's not that,' Henry replied.

'I understand. But the people I know, they don't trust too. If I bring you to them, they angry. It's up to you, maybe you find someone to buy before the duke find you.' Lucia sounded nonchalant but clearly she had figured out that Henry had taken the bird from the duke and did not exactly have his blessing for this trip to Venice. Lucia was sharp and far more streetwise than those sweet eyes let on; she probably did know some top priggers. Lucia reached in and kissed Henry again.

'I will sell and come to Venice with you?' Lucia said. Henry pictured them in a luxury cabin of a grand boat sailing the Mediterranean Sea, bound for Venice. Yet Mary suddenly came to Henry's mind, accompanied by guilt he could not understand. *She betrayed you; forget her.*

Henry reached into his pocket and handed Lucia the bird. She took it from the pouch and held it up to the light, examining it for flaws the way Henry had seen jewellers do.

'There is a ship that leaves at twelve tomorrow. Opposite the dock is a bousing ken called the Bull's Head. Can you meet me there in the morning?' Henry asked.

'Yes,' Lucia replied, still looking at the bird.

'Are you sure you want to come with me?' he asked. Lucia did not respond.

'Lucia, are you *sure* you want to come?' Henry asked again.

Lucia shook her head like she was waking from a trance. She put the bird back in its pouch and tucked the pouch into her dress. She kissed Henry once more. 'I am sure.'

Henry did not know if he felt relief, but he knew this was his best option – his only *real* option, perhaps.

He wrapped his arms around her, savouring the smell of her neck, his desire heightened by fear.

'I am sorry, I must go, but I will see you tomorrow,' Henry said, looking into Lucia's eyes to search for honesty.

'Yes, twelve I come to Bull's Head.'

Henry trotted down the stairs and closed the door behind him without looking back.

As he walked back out on to the Southside, Henry spotted the same group of young boys that he had seen before. They were looking among the rubbish where Henry had been hidden.

'Oi!' Henry called and beckoned them over to him.

He knew it was foolish – he hardly had money to spare – but

he remembered the terrible pangs of hunger that had driven him to look through people's rubbish so many times. Henry took two pennies from his pocket and held his hand out to the boy who'd walked over.

'Get a nice loaf for you and your mates.'

The young boy looked at Henry with the confused suspicion of someone who had never been given anything for free. He reached out slowly with a grubby hand and snatched the money from Henry's palm. The boy ran back towards his friends and Henry smiled as he began his walk down Southside.

Henry walked quickly and purposefully, keeping his head down and his hood up. Occasionally, he raised his eyes to see who and what was around – but without ever lifting his head. He had the sudden urge to do so many things: go up to the roof of St Paul's and admire the view, swim in the Thames, watch the bears and the bulls and a play. All for the last time.

Romeville. Henry knew how much this place was a part of him. *Will I ever feel that way about Venice?* he wondered as he arrived at the inn.

The Bull's Head was a typical sailor's inn. Rough and dirty, filled with foreigners and doxies, a place where no questions were asked. You'd be lucky if you heard two words of English spoken here all day. It was one of the few places in London where a foreigner, even a black one, would not arouse much notice, much less suspicion. Henry ordered a meat pie, a pint of ale and room for the night, and settled down for a long wait.

Henry's mother walked into Lucia's apartment. She lifted up the bed with one hand and it flew into the air, like Joan holding Agnes with a chi shot. She held her other hand out horizontally and several floorboards sprang up, exposing the rats running around underneath, eating whatever they could find, including each other. She pulled down the wall drapes to expose the rotten walls beneath and they crumbled around her, yet stayed standing, crumbling over and over again in a constant stream, like the flow of the Thames. Lucia came dancing into the room like a ballerina, dressed in her finest clothes. Henry's mother danced with her, holding her like a male partner. As Lucia leaned over in the dance, Henry's mother dug her nails in to Lucia's face, drawing blood instantly, but Lucia did not scream.

Even in his sleep, Henry felt his body jump at the sight, but his mother only dug her nails in further, blood pouring from Lucia's cheeks now. She squeezed ever tighter, pulling Lucia's face off and carrying her flapping skin in her hand. Underneath Lucia's face was not flesh but insects, pests, flies — the kinds that gathered around shit and bit people, making them sick.

She casts a spell over the boy to keep him invisible from Elegba. Again she goes, leaving her child behind, but taking the curse with her.

18

His room in the inn had no windows but from the sound of the cocks crowing and the noise of people coming into town from Kent, Henry could tell that the sun had risen. Every morning a deluge of farmers and traders queued up along the road into London, ready to burst into the city as soon as the gates opened. Henry imagined the endless stream of carts loaded with strawberries and pears, potatoes, chickens and milk lining up out there.

He lay still for a moment as he heard the dock come alive on the other side of the building. Sailors shouted in the typical dockside mix of French, German, Italian and English. Planks creaked under the weight of feet; he heard the pull of ropes and the clash of chains. *Today is the day*, he told himself with a shiver.

He'd spent all night juggling dreams of himself and Lucia on the high seas and fear that he'd been scammed by the oldest trick in the book – a beautiful doxy. Unable to bear being alone with his thoughts any longer, he ventured downstairs for breakfast. Even at this early hour, the pub was full with men smoking pipes, drinking and playing cards. Henry ordered a meat pie at the bar and sat in a corner seat, looking out of the window at the ships outside.

And there it was, *The Merchant Royal* – a beautiful four-hundred-ton monster of a ship, shining dark brown because it was newly made, its sails the blinding white of cloth not aged by decades of voyages. *Today is the day*, Henry repeated to himself, unable to keep his leg from shaking – whether from excitement, nerves or fear, he could not say. He looked from the ship to the pub door and back again, just waiting on the moment that Lucia would arrive with her smile and his money. Last night's dream flashed before him and he felt his mother's energy.

He watched as gangs of men and boys that couldn't have been much older than seven unloaded the mountain of crates from the ship – a ritual happening not just here, but on several ships along the dockside. Then the boat was empty and the sun was rising in the sky, peeking out from behind spring clouds. The men soon started again but in the opposite direction, unloading from the dock's storehouse and on to the ship, until another mountain of boxes and crates covered the deck.

Two black sailors caught Henry's eye and he watched them at work, thinking about the famous pirates of Barbary and the Moors in Spain. He wondered if the men came from the same place as his mother. *Maybe they even know her*, he thought, then laughed at himself for his own silliness.

He looked up at the sun. It was nearly midday, yet still no sign of Lucia. More flashes of last night's dream. He desperately needed to pee but could not bear to get up from the table for even one moment, lest he miss her.

She will be here any minute, she will be here soon, it was just a dream, he repeated to himself over and over.

Henry ran back through the instructions he had given her, sure that he had been clear. Had something happened to her? One of the famous sonnets about night women crept into his mind.

> *The woman of the night trust not young man*
> *Lest your pockets become light as you sleep*
> *Stay out of her grip be gone while you can*
> *All that you sow she doth intend to reap*

Not Lucia, Henry, he told himself. *She'll be here any minute.* But the sonnet would not stop its taunt.

> *Woman of the night: devil of the day*
> *She that is guided by lust is a trap*
> *For joy and delight you surely shall pay*
> *More than the price of the goods on display*

Henry thought of the look on Lucia's face as she held the golden bird up to the light, as she practically begged him to let her sell it in her broken English. Even that was probably just a scam to sound cute. *Oh, the sin of woman*, Henry thought remembering everything he'd learned in church.

Over at the dockside, the captain walked aboard the ship and started the final preparations before departure. The sails were untied; the ship was almost ready to leave.

Henry fingered the remaining coins Graham had given him. It certainly wasn't enough to buy passage. Maybe he could beg the captain to let him work for the cost of his travel. But he'd barely be able to eat and he did not want to travel so destitute, not when just last night he'd had in his hands a golden bird worth a few years' wages. He had to wait for her. The anchor was pulled from the sea and heaved aboard the ship by the gang of sailors.

She would not betray me, would she? Something might have happened to her . . . But Matthew betrayed you, Joan betrayed you . . . your own mother left you, you worthless idiot. How could you be so stupid as to trust a doxy you had only met once with a priceless object . . .

Henry watched as the plank was drawn up. This was his last chance – he could run now and maybe the captain would allow one last straggler.

Get up, Henry. Just go. Lucia is not coming.

His bladder was about to explode, but Henry's feet would not carry him anywhere. He was fixed to his seat, unable to take his eyes from the ship for a split second, as if he somehow expected Lucia to jump off it at any moment and surprise him.

With a shout, the sailors untied the great vessel and it pulled away from the dock, following the tide. Slowly, torturously, the big ship turned and made its way out into the Thames, gathering speed until it eventually faded from Henry's sight. Tears streamed down Henry's face, stopping in the hairs of his newly emerging beard. He wiped away the moisture, steadied himself and got up to go to the toilet. As his bladder exhaled relief, Henry reached a decision.

Forget everyone.

He'd had enough. He would not torture himself by looking for Lucia. Clearly, she had decided not to come. She had sold his golden bird and kept the money for herself like the little scheming doxy that she was. Henry would do what he did best: pick a few pockets to get the money for passage and leave London forever. *Like I should have done years ago.*

There was another boat leaving for Venice in two days. All he had to do was keep safe until then. Thinking of Moll Cutpurse's poem, he would go back to his room and rest until tomorrow.

> *The tired thief in hunger for his bread*
> *Becomes so sloppy he loses his head.*
> *Thou art too tired? The best cure is bed*
> *All men can sleep but can't eat once they're dead*

Henry ordered a bottle of strong wine and another meat pie. He returned to his room, knowing the money Graham had given him was fast running out. Even if he hadn't wanted to leave London, Henry would have had no choice but to steal again soon. He drank the wine in large gulps. It was cheap, harsh-tasting stuff, nothing like the delicate wines he had got used to at the duke's house, but it did the job. Soon Henry's head was spinning and tiredness came over his body. He took his mother's letter out from his pocket and just stared at it, reading the single line over and over again, until he fell asleep.

A crowd ran riot, horses' hooves crushed bodies, a woman lay on the floor, dead. A grief grabbed Henry's body so totally he wished he could wake up. His mother appeared, but not as a presence that imposed itself on his dreams – Henry could feel himself creating this image as he slept. She was sitting around a feast table rather like the duke's, only grander. She was surrounded by Venetian high society but dressed like one of the English noblewomen he had seen picnicking on top of St Paul's, a silk mask covering her face, black skin and curly hair peeking through at the top. Her guests were laughing and drinking copious amounts of wine.

'How is the boy?' She said it not as a question, but as a joke. Her guests laughed in Henry's face like the group on the roof of St Paul's, only more menacingly.

'How is the boy?' She said it again, and again laughter.

'How is the boy?' The guests around the table started to join in, chanting the words as they looked at Henry directly, through his mind's eye.

How is the boy?

How is the boy?

How is the boy?

Henry woke from his dream, his head splitting from the cheap wine. He tried to dismiss it as just another meaningless fantasy, but he couldn't.

What if Joan was telling the truth? What if my mother does not want to know me and I throw away my life here to find her?

Then he remembered his decision: *Forget everyone. So what if my mother does not want me? I can't spend the rest of my life wondering what if. I need to know.*

Henry got dressed, picked up his bag and hit the streets. It was time to get his money the only way he knew how.

He stormed out of the pub, pushing the doors so hard that they swung open wildly and rebounded, almost hitting him in the face. He marched up Southside, past the southern gate and a fresh set of severed heads, and on to London Bridge. He was half-way along before his stride started to calm.

Henry began scouting for victims. He walked towards a large queue at one of the houses up ahead – stationary people were always easier to pickpocket than moving ones.

He peered through the window of the house to see what all the fuss was about and saw a strange-looking animal with a long neck, a huge lump on its back and hair the colour of sand. *The animal has a face like a grumpy old man*, Henry thought. This was Mr Jones's Curiosity Shop, he realised. A place that was said to contain all the wonders of the Indies and beyond. Mr Jones himself had travelled half the world and brought back these many curiosities. How had he not sought out this place before now?

He joined the queue and asked the man in front of him what the animal in the window was.

'I believe it is called a camel.' The man had a pleasant face and Henry did not really want to rob him, but there would be few opportunities this easy. *Forget everyone, remember?*

'A camel. What a strange creature. Where is it from?' Henry asked.

'I don't know. Some have said Egypt. You can never be sure with Mr Jones. You have to take what he tells you with a pinch of salt. He has been known to . . . embellish . . . his stories from time to time.'

As he spoke, Henry slipped his hand into the man's pocket and took his purse.

'They say the animal has magical powers,' the man went on, 'and to touch it will bring great fortunes.'

'Amazing! How I wish I could stay and see it today, but this queue is moving very slowly and I have errands to run for my master. Adieu, friend.' Henry tipped his hat at the man.

'Adieu,' the man replied.

Henry walked around the stalls on the bridge, perusing the fruits and meats and leather wallets. He picked a pocket at the apple stand, another by the fishmonger and yet another from a man who was birdwatching over the Thames.

He noticed something curious: when he had stolen wearing the poor ragged clothes of a commoner, people were constantly on guard and most would not even allow him to get close. But now, with the expensive cast-offs of Duke Wilmslow, people looked at him with respect. He saw them notice his colour, then his clothes – or his clothes and then his colour – and their eyes did the calculation right there in front of him.

Yes, you are brown, but to be dressed like that you must be connected to somebody important.

The nobility's recent penchant for exotic black servants was known by all, so even people who were otherwise revolted by his skin looked at him with a grudging respect. Troubling a noble's servant was harming his property – an offence punishable by death.

Henry picked one more pocket – while helping a woman to carry her bags to her cart – then decided he'd move on to another location. He was surprised that he did not feel guilty.

Forget everyone.

He walked off and counted his money. He still did not have enough for his passage, and how would he eat on the journey, let alone survive once he got to Venice? Henry wanted to get as close as possible to the small fortune that the bird would have brought him. He walked over the north side of the bridge and turned towards the inns of court: the law students and clerks were notoriously easy to rob. Henry picked three more pockets. Some even tipped their hats to him.

Eight pockets, Henry said to himself. That was a lot for a few hours' work, even by his standards, and should be enough to haggle a deal with the captain. He decided it was best to go back to the inn and keep his head low, in case he got sloppy. But then Henry caught a whiff of sweet bread that churned his stomach and realised there was one more thing he had to do before he turned his back on this city forever.

Henry saw the same ugly thin-faced man behind the bakery counter and smiled to himself; the first time he had smiled all day. He waltzed into the bakery as if he owned the place, adjusting his cloak in exaggerated moves.

Henry got to the front of the queue and looked the man straight in his face. The shock and anger in the man's eyes was almost poetic – an image that Henry had no doubt would stay with him his whole life.

'Two fresh white, one granary, two sweet tarts and a jar of honey please,' Henry said.

The server stared at Henry, his nose and cheeks growing red as the man fought to suppress his anger. If only he knew that Henry was bluffing, that Henry was not connected to a rich and powerful duke, that he was actually on the run from the duke who had given him these clothes. It gave Henry an even sweeter taste of victory. Nobody would be foolish enough to risk getting put into the stocks for something so trivial as refusing a noble's servant.

The man reached back and got Henry his loaves, his honey and his pastries. Henry took his things with a wide obnoxious smile and handed the man the money. 'Keep the change,' he added.

He moved to the side to allow the next person to order and opened one of his loaves right there on the counter, and also his jar of honey. He dipped the bread in, making a mess of crumbs and honey on the counter as he ate.

'I say, this is some fine, fine bread you have, and the honey is delightful,' Henry said, knowing that using pompous terms like 'delightful' would help to rub the man's face in it.

Henry watched the man battle with his anger, staying by the counter until half the loaf was gone, then smacking his lips and licking his fingers as loudly as he could.

'Good day, sir, be well,' Henry said to the man and left the shop feeling elated. Sure, the pain of Joan and Lucia and Matthew all betraying him would return soon enough, but for now, he felt good.

Outside the bakers, Henry noticed a small boy staring at him from across the street. Something in it made him uneasy; the boy was not looking with the same reverence that people seemed to have for Henry now, but as if he could see through Henry's act. The boy had bright blond hair, so light it was almost white, and piercing blue eyes that put Henry on edge. He stared back, but the boy did not look away.

Henry quickened his pace and turned down a back alley that he knew well, taking a few twists and turns and coming out on to Cheapside. Henry glanced behind him, his heart racing with fear, but there was nobody there. *Stop being so paranoid, Henry*.

Henry walked the rest of the journey swiftly, but not so fast as to attract attention. He had reached the southern gate and went to turn left towards The Bull's Head when he saw a little body duck behind an apple cart in the corner of his vision, the bright blond hair moving like a flash. Henry did not know what to do. Maybe it was nothing and just paranoia playing tricks on him, maybe it was a trap, but it could also be Lucia or Graham trying to send him a message. Henry's feet carried him towards the apple cart. He felt his heart and breathing stop, his head screaming at him to run the other way, but his legs walked on stubbornly towards the cart. Henry braced himself, bent down and looked . . . there was nothing there.

She visits the boy in the spirit world as much as she can,

gives him gifts and talents that he cannot understand,

but in the land of strangers, the man child – grandson

of the cursed general from the kingdom of Benin –

will have to find his own way.

19

Henry came down from bed intending to order breakfast and an ale then go back to his room until it was time to leave. He took a seat at the bar and beckoned for the server's attention. The smell of beer and eggs and burned sausages mixed with the smoke from tobacco pipes gave the air a faint grey tinge and a scent that was both musty and sweet. While waiting for the server to come over, Henry scanned the faces of the people around him.

By Solomon, it can't be.

On the opposite side of the room was a face Henry knew. Of all the people to be in here on the day he intended to leave London forever, there he was: Matthew, sat alone, staring into a glass.

It was definitely him.

His clothes looked better but he was still as pork-faced as ever.

I bet he is still spending the lour the duke gave him to grass on me.

Henry breathed heavily through his nose like a small child who has just been told off. None of the positive memories mattered any more as he stared at Matthew. That was the boy that had got him beaten and imprisoned in the duke's dungeon, the boy that had betrayed every code of thievery and friendship, the boy that had caused Henry's life to take the turns that it had. Without him, Henry would have never met Lucia and been so brutally betrayed again. That was the boy that had lost him the golden bird. Henry thought of Hamlet's speech.

To be, or not to be: that is the question:
Whether 'tis nobler in the mind to suffer
The slings and arrows of outrageous fortune,
Or to take arms against a sea of troubles
And, by opposing, end them?

Henry did not want to *suffer the slings and arrows of outrageous fortune*; he wanted revenge. He wanted to punch Matthew even harder than before. He wanted to see him scream and yelp in pain like a little girl, his nose and eyes swollen under the weight of punches. Yet Henry knew that he could not *take up arms against a sea of troubles*; he could not afford to attract that much attention.

But he had to get revenge somehow. He could not let Matthew get away with it.

'Hello?' The server disturbed Henry's thoughts. Henry wondered how long he had been standing there.

'I'll take the breakfast and a pint of ale please.' Henry reached into his pocket to get his purse and felt a glass vial. It took him a moment to remember what it was and then Graham's voice came to him.

Do not drink wine before or after you take it. You'll crap your

278

guts out if you do.

There it was. Henry might not be able to beat Matthew like he deserved to be beaten, but he would do something much worse.

'And a bottle of Rome-bouse, please,' Henry added, sliding the coins across the bar.

'Your food will be out in a minute.' The server handed Henry his bottle of wine and began to pour his ale.

'Thanks, I'll be over there.' Henry gestured to the seats by the window where he had watched the ship leave two days ago. He would be out of the view of Matthew there, the corner side of the bar blocking the way. He uncorked the bottle, poured half the vial's contents in and re-corked it as fast as possible. He wrote a small note and stuck it to the bottle.

Thanks for everything.

The server brought out Henry's food and he wolfed it down quickly. Soon enough the server was back to collect his empty cup and slab.

'Say, mate,' Henry said as the server cleared the table. 'I spotted an old friend of mine across the bar and I'd like to surprise him. Could you give him this bottle for me? I'll be back soon. It's the fat lad with the grey cap on. Matthew is his name.' Henry slipped a coin across the table to sweeten the deal.

'Yes, sir. Who shall I say it is from?'

'The duke,' Henry replied without thinking. He smiled to himself, pleased with the poetic touch, and got up to walk out on to the river front.

Henry imagined Matthew sitting on the bar stool, crapping

his pants all over the floor. He imagined walking back in and laughing in Matthew's face as he gripped his stomach and tried to run for the jakes, skid-marks sailing down the back of his breeches. Of course, he would not get that pleasure – letting Matthew know he was still in town when he was so close to getting away was absolutely stupid – but the imagining alone gave him some joy.

Outside, Henry drew a deep breath. Oh, how he'd be glad to be rid of that stink.

He wondered what Venice smelled like, picturing the wonders of the floating city and ignoring what Lucia had said.

The Southside was itself, even in the morning: commerce and cunning, peasants and prostitutes. Spring was fighting to arrive. It was a pleasant morning, with a chill in the air and the sun battling through the clouds. Henry did not want to venture too far from the port and risk being seen, so he sat on a pile of crates that overlooked the Thames and started playing with sonnets in his head.

> *Lucia so sweet to touch and the eye*
> *Wish never had I glanced on thy fine face*
> *A fool to trust what my senses do guide*
> *How men's desires often lead to disg—*

Henry was interrupted by the sight of a young woman walking down towards the Bull's Head. She was pretty and curvy, her dark hair long and thick. She drew closer, and the freckles on her smooth skin looked familiar.

By Solomon . . . it can't be.

But he was sure it was her and he was panicked. *Why is she here? It can't be a coincidence.*

Before Henry had a chance to decide what to do, she saw him too. He could not read the look in her eyes but she carried on walking towards him.

'May I?' she asked, pointing to the space on the crates next to Henry.

Henry grunted and nodded. She sat down.

He looked out at the Thames, waiting for Mary to apologise, but she did not speak. The seconds turned to minutes and Henry's anger grew. He desperately wanted to turn his head to get another look at her, but tried to resist.

Henry just could not hold in his words any more. 'So, you're not even gonna say sorry?' Henry demanded.

'I was gonna ask you the same question,' Mary replied.

The cheek of it, Henry thought. Yes, he'd been a jolt-head, but that was nothing compared to what she'd done. Yet she wanted him to apologise. An image of Mary, helpless, hanging by her feet from the duke's window came to him. He thought about the future that could have been if they'd got away from the duke's that night.

'All this – the way things have turned out – it's your fault,' Henry said, looking up the river, still turned away from Mary. 'If you had just bloody well jumped from the window that night instead of acting like a scared little girl, we'd have got away and

281

everything would have been different.'

'I did wonder when you'd throw that one back at me. Well, at least you've got it off your chest. Still don't explain why you became such a jolt-head to me the moment Wilmslow gave you a nice pair of breeches.' Mary sounded stronger than Henry remembered and even through his anger, he liked it.

'I think deep down I always knew.'

'Knew what?' Mary asked.

Henry turned and looked Mary squarely in the eyes. He wanted her to feel what he was about to say. 'Knew that all of you could not be trusted.'

Mary went to speak but then stopped herself.

'I leave today, forever,' Henry continued. 'Wilmslow is after me and I have no one I can trust or turn to, so I'm gone.'

'Yeah, Graham told me. Where you going, then?'

It seemed Mary was not rising to the bait. Henry could not work out why. It irritated him that she was not arguing back and it irritated him even more that she looked so beautiful.

'Venice, obviously.'

'Why *obviously*?'

'Are you joking?'

'What do you mean?'

'Don't take me for an idiot, Mary.'

'What?'

'You really don't know?'

'Know *what*?'

Henry stared into Mary's face, trying to find signs of bluffing, but there were none.

'Joan knew my mother was alive and she decided not to tell me. My mother is in Venice.'

'Pish,' Mary said. 'Joan would not do that.'

'I have the letter my mum wrote to Joan.'

Mary looked at Henry for a few searching seconds. 'So that's—'

A sailor walked past them, close enough to hear their conversation, and Mary paused.

'Can I help you, friend?' she asked the sailor, her voice impressively gruff and assertive. He took the hint and walked on quickly.

'*That's* what she meant,' Mary continued. 'Joan is on her way here. When I told her you were leaving, she said she had to see you. There was something off about how she said it.'

A scream erupted from the pub.

'Somebody call a physician!'

As Henry remembered what he had done to Matthew, he half-laughed. A commotion started, with more and more people crowding around the pub and looking through the windows.

Another person emerged from the pub, shouting, 'Physician, physician! We need a physician!'

The next moment, Matthew was carried out like a wounded soldier and Henry froze.

He only said it would make you crap yourself.

'Matthew!' Mary shouted, running towards him, Henry following.

'Give him some air! Don't crowd around!' The people who'd carried Matthew out of the pub placed him on the floor. He was vomiting and foaming at the mouth, his eyes rolling back in his head as if he were having a fit.

The guilt almost knocked Henry off his feet. He wanted to run, though he knew his legs would not move, no matter how much he wanted them to. Surely everyone could see the guilt written on his face?

'Matthew!' Mary screamed, her voice desperate. She fell to the ground next to her brother and fear pulled Henry down beside her.

You stupid idiot! Why hadn't he just got on the boat and quietly sailed away? Why had he been such a little kid and tried to give Matthew the runs? *Look what you have done now.*

Matthew jolted and jerked. Henry heard him struggling for breath as he choked on his own vomit and wished that he could somehow turn back time and undo what he'd done.

The crowd around Matthew was growing by the second. His eyes bulged, his face turned purple, his lungs grabbed at the air . . .

And then he just stopped cold.

Henry could not process what he had just seen. Mary let out a scream so visceral that it seemed to push the crowd back. *You caused this.*

Henry felt a strong energy and the force of someone pushing forward. A second later, Joan emerged from among the crowd of bodies. The people nearby moved back as if they felt something in Joan's aura; Henry could feel that she was using a mild version of the *chi* shot.

Joan did not seem to notice anyone but Matthew, her eyes focused and calm, as if she were alone in a room with only him. She still looked old but far less frail somehow, her movements direct and purposeful. She took out a crystal from her undergarments and placed it against Matthew's heart, pushing down multiple times while chanting an incantation in her native language. Again and again, she pushed and chanted, the crystal lighting up and shining a warm blue energy through the back of her hand and into Matthew's chest.

Please, God, Henry prayed to himself, *help Joan save Matthew and I swear I'll never do something so stupid again.*

Matthew did not stir. Mary continued to scream, the sound of her cry so demented that Henry knew it would stay with him forever. It had never occurred to him just how much Mary loved her big brother until now. Joan kept working, chanting her incantation and pushing down through the light of the crystal, on to Matthew's heart. The light changed her, made her seem like the old Joan: strong and full of life, her face peaceful and plain, the wrinkles less pronounced.

She took a vial of liquid from her bag and poured it into Matthew's mouth while continuing to push on his chest. Still, Matthew did not stir. Henry looked round to see a huge crowd had now gathered, all staring at Joan as she held the shining crystal and chanted in some foreign Gypsy tongue.

As Henry turned back to Matthew, the boy coughed and

spluttered, sitting up as if he had been jolted from the realms of the dead. His face was even more transparent than usual with purple and blue blotches discolouring his pink skin. His hair was caked in vomit and dirt and the look on his face suggested he had absolutely no idea where he was. A relief came over Henry that was even more intense than his feelings of guilt. He could barely breathe, feeling dizzy and utterly drained.

'Witch!' someone in the crowd shouted.

Henry's relief vanished. He closed his eyes and prayed to God that it would not catch on.

'She's a bloody witch – a Gyptian witch.'

Henry spun round to look for the voice.

'She used dark magic to bring that boy back from the dead.'

It was a man with a spotty, contorted face. The cruel look in his eyes reminded Henry of the baker's son.

'Witch, witch, witch!' the crowd started chanting.

Henry glared at them, praying they would be quiet and go away, but all he could see on their faces was hatred and fear and a lust for blood. He thought of Billy's battered, swollen face and the way he'd disappeared into a sea of bodies just like this one and come out of it dead. He remembered the monkey and the mob – the way they'd torn that little animal limb from limb and likely would have destroyed each other if the Queen's guards had not come.

Henry felt something stronger than fear flood his veins and it took him a moment to understand what it was. Powerlessness. You could be scared of one man or two, but there was a good chance you could get away or even defend yourself. What was the point in being scared of a hundred people? With shared intentions they could do to you whatever they wanted.

A large stone whipped through the air and struck Joan in her ribs. She was clearly winded but held firm and struggled to help Matthew to his feet. Another stone lashed her in the shoulder; a rotten apple flew past her cheek. Henry jumped in the way and tried to shield Joan, but it was futile – random objects had started to fly from all directions. Joan let out a *chi* shot that pushed a few of the closest people away, but this only made things worse.

'Oi, that witch just pushed me without even touching me!' the spotty man shouted.

The crowd swarmed in. Hands began grabbing Joan, pulling her in different directions. Somehow she retained the calm emotionless look on her face as she tugged the hands off her clothes and pushed the people back. Henry fought to reach her, wildly shoving anyone in his way.

She soon disappeared from view, into the storm of bodies. Every so often a wave of energy would shoot through the crowd, pushing more people back, and Henry would know that Joan was still conscious.

But how long can she last?

He strode forward to search for her but the weight of the crowd tipped him off balance, the soles of his shoes slipping on a wet patch of stone. Feet trampled over him, each blow bruising his face and ribs. He fought to stand up, but was pushed back

287

down, again and again, by wet, muddy feet stampeding towards the action. He struggled to breathe as heat and darkness suffocated him, beams of sunlight flashing through the legs of people as they shoved past. His lungs ripped at the air with everything they had, but he could not draw enough breath to satisfy them. His chest burned and his head began to pound.

'Kill the witch, kill the witch, kill the witch!' the crowd chanted in unison.

Henry heard the loud sound of glass smashing and guessed the pub windows must be gone.

Where is Joan? Where is Mary?

The crowd seemed to pause for a second, giving Henry a chance to get up. He pulled at someone's leg and used their body as leverage to stand. He looked out across the crowd and could not believe how far he had been carried by the mob in just a few moments.

All hell had broken loose: some people were fighting each other, others were running into shops and stealing or turning over carts of produce or smashing windows. It was developing into a full-scale riot.

'Kill the witch, burn the witch, torch the witch!' many were still chanting.

Henry could not see Mary, Joan or Matthew.

He pushed through the bodies closest to him, barging people like he was on the football field. 'Get out of my way!' Henry shouted like a madman. A couple of people cleared him a path but most were still rushing blindly towards the action.

He kept pushing and shoving but he was going nowhere fast. For each movement forward he was carried backwards again by the bodies.

Drums sounded and everybody froze. The looks of glee and bloodlust on people's faces were immediately replaced by fear.

The drums pounded again and people started running in random directions, bumping into one another on the way. Henry heard the clatter of hooves in the distance, quickly growing louder until it became a torrent of noise. He looked round to see scores of mounted horses coming towards them, then the parish constable and his men galloped into the crowd. They swung their clubs at the heads of the rioters, knocking men and women out cold. The horses trampled through the bodies. Some people ran off down side streets, some jumped over the small wall on to the banks of the Thames, some were crushed under hooves.

A horseman came charging towards Henry, his club lifted, ready to strike. Henry tried to jump out of the way as the club swung down, but it was too late. It slammed into his shoulder, sending a crack through his entire body. Henry fell to the floor in agony, his shoulder burning with pain, each small movement hurting like hell.

He pulled himself to his feet slowly, his stomach queasy from the pain. The chaos was still raging – men tucked their stolen produce into their clothes and fled; ladies walked towards the mounted soldiers seeking help, their dresses torn and their hair caked with mud and dirt; gentlemen looked forlorn, having been stripped of their outer garments and jewels. The tensions, superstitions and resentments of London had been vomited out on this street to devastating effect and it was all Henry's fault.

Why had he been so childish?

Within a short time though, much of the crowd was gone. A few had been arrested and the constable's men were already wheeling in a set of stocks and a hanging post to make quick examples of some of the worst offenders. People were scattered across the ground, some with broken bones, others looking half-dead, some yelping in pain.

Among it all, finally, he saw them.

On the spot outside the pub where Matthew had lain, Mary was crouched over Joan, crying hysterically. Henry ran towards them. Joan's body lay sprawled out, her clothes torn and her head bleeding profusely. Henry knelt down and rubbed Mary on her back with his good arm, his guilt burning more than the pain. Mary turned and buried her head in Henry's chest, sobbing so hard it vibrated through his body. Henry felt sick, bile rising to his throat. He could not possibly bring himself to tell her this was all his fault. Instead, he hugged Mary and stroked her back again.

'Somebody get a barber-surgeon!' Henry screamed through his tears.

Nobody even looked in his direction. The constable's men were far too busy administering on-the-spot punishments to worry about helping injured people.

Joan said something that Henry could not make out. He put his ear near her mouth.

'I'm sorry, Henry,' Joan whispered. 'Your mother does love you, I promise.' The gash on her head had left a large pool of blood and her hair was soaked with red. Her face was bashed in and bruised and her arms contorted in such a way that it was clear they were both broken.

Henry let go of Mary and held Joan. Mary rubbed his back now. As he looked down at the woman who had taken him in as a little boy, tears dripping from his face, Joan's eyes turned cold and lifeless. She stopped breathing, right there in Henry's arms. Images of his life with Joan flashed across Henry's mind: the cold winters, her warm soups, the stale bread shared, the times she had cured him of sickness with her potions or fought with Agnes on his behalf. He saw them in the special room, working on a translation, and then the argument about his mother.

Henry started wailing but pulled back a breath when he saw the server he had given the bottle of wine to in the distance. He was talking to one of the constable's men when he caught Henry's eye.

'Mary, we've got to leave,' Henry said, letting go of Joan's body.

'What? We can't just leave her here like this,' Mary replied through her tears.

'I've just seen one of the duke's spies,' Henry lied. 'We have to go. I'm sorry.'

The server pointed at Henry, and Henry's whole body went cold. He pulled at Mary's sleeve.

'I'm sorry Mary, we have to go.'

But Mary just would not budge; she was staring at Joan, crying and trying to breathe. The server and the officer started to walk towards them.

'Mary!' Henry shouted and pulled again at her sleeve. He felt sick inside, tearing Mary away from her dead aunt like this, a death he had caused. The men got closer.

Mary bolted up as if she had just registered Henry's words about the duke's spies. They ran. Henry and Mary ran without even looking back to see if any of the constable's men had followed them. They ran for their lives, sprinting west down the dockside, past the bridge and through alley after back alley, pushing passers-by, jumping over crates and dodging sewage, until they came to a part of Southside Henry had never seen before. Maybe it was the unfamiliar surroundings but more likely it was the grief and guilt, but Henry just could not go on. He remembered his shoulder injury and suddenly it throbbed again violently, overwhelming his senses.

'Why you stopping?' Mary asked, panting.

'I can't go any more. I just can't.'

'Over there.' Mary pointed to a side street. Henry tried to follow her as she ran, but Mary had to support him so that he would not collapse. They were now far away from the riot but there still were stragglers carrying their stolen goods, their bodies patched with wounds, talking excitedly about the battle.

Henry sat on the stony ground as they hid in the alley and tried to process what had just happened.

Did Joan really just die in my arms?

Visions of Matthew coughing and spluttering and dying and Joan bringing him back to life flooded Henry's head. He was haunted by the memory of Mary's visceral scream and of Joan, dead. He had caused all of this.

Mary's voice stirred him from his sorrows. 'What we gonna do, Henry?'

'I don't know!' Henry's pain was so deep that he couldn't even cry. It was like his body had stopped working properly. 'I have to leave. London is not safe for me.'

'I'll come with you,' Mary said.

'So, what do we do?' Henry asked, as if Mary coming was just common sense.

'You said the ship was leaving today?'

'Ay.'

'I'll go down to the docks and see if I can buy us passage. Then I'll come back to get you.'

Henry took some money out of his purse. Mary nodded and took it. 'It's going to be all right,' she said. 'They'll be too busy looking for rioters now to look for you. I'll be back sooner than you think.'

'Mary?'

'Yes, Henry?'

'Thank you.'

Mary turned and walked off round the corner.

Henry waited, replaying the incidents of the last week over and over. Lucia and their romance; her lips, her touch. She had taken the golden bird from his hand, smiling and pretending to care, and then had disappeared. Would Mary do the same? Henry wondered what had happened to Matthew. He saw the life drain from Joan's eyes over and over again.

Each second felt like an hour. The cold ground had deadened his buttocks, yet he could not bring himself to get up despite the rats running around his feet and the sewage floating past him. His Spanish leather shoes were caked in filth, several buttons on his shirt had popped and his cloak was ripped, but none of that mattered now.

Come on, Mary, come back now.

Come on, Mary, please.

Henry thought about the duke and Dr Dee and the society. He wondered if that life would have been so bad after all. He remembered the warm baths, the full bellies and when he had first slid on this pair of Spanish leather shoes. Maybe he really was a spoiled little fool for leaving a life like that, as Graham had said.

He thought of his dreams and the strange way his mother's image had tried to guide him through them. He had to see her. He had to get to Venice. But for now he had to get out of London, alive.

Come on, Mary, please.

'She'll be back soon,' Henry told himself out loud, looking at the sun. Henry saw himself as a young boy being dragged from the Thames, coughing up water and waste, with Joan pushing on his chest the same way she had just pushed on Matthew's. He had killed the very woman that had saved his life. The guilt made him feel a weakness he had never known before, like he had no control over his body at all; like his bowels or bladder might empty themselves and he could do nothing; like his legs might not move, even if he wanted them to.

A new terror pulled at Henry's insides as he looked across the street and saw the piercing blue eyes staring back at him. The little blond phantom that, until now, Henry had half-thought he was imagining. The child tilted its head, beckoning.

Henry felt the blow to the back of his own head a split second before things went black. A cloth bag was pulled tight as two sets of hands held his arms and another grabbed his legs, pulling him up from the ground and carrying him. Henry struggled and tried to shout but the cloth was too thick, the hands gripping him far too strong for him to have any hope of breaking free – but still he struggled. He cried to himself, cursing his own wretched stupidity. Why had he believed he could ever get away? Why did he have to get his silly revenge on Matthew and draw so much attention to himself? Who had caught him? Was it the duke's men or the constable's? Would he be killed now as punishment? Henry was not sure that he feared death anymore. What was the point of living if he'd never get to see the world, to see his mother? But he did fear torture.

Henry did not know how far he'd been carried when the men holding him put him down and held him still. They tied up his hands with rope, burning his wrists with their violent yanks, before picking him back up and folding him like linen, squeezing his arms and legs together. Henry felt himself being dumped into a crate. He could tell a lid had been placed over him by the way the sound changed. A time passed in silence. Henry did not know if it was an hour or a minute, but he was annoyed with himself for bothering to notice the scent of spring in the air, and the faint ring of a church bell when he was about to die.

Henry felt something drop into the crate, then a strange smell struck his nose and he immediately knew that it was some kind of poison. He held his breath, trying not to breathe in the acrid smell, hoping against hope that someone would open the crate and save him. Of all the things to do, why would the duke or the constable kill him like this? So secretly, so simply. Poison? Poison was a woman's weapon. A witch's weapon. *Agnes* . . .

Henry held until his lungs felt like they were going to explode through his stomach, and he gasped a large lungful of the horrible smell. His eyes watered and started to become heavy. As he drifted off into death all he could think about was his mother. He was grateful that his end had been painless at least.

Henry awoke to the feeling of swaying. The bed he slept on was comfortable; the walls around him looked like a small wooden cabin. He took in the unmistakable sound of waves and the noises from outside the door, and he slowly realised that he was on a ship. He sat up and looked around the room. His cloak had been hung on the back of the door and his shoes placed neatly beside the bed. A solitary envelope sat on a wooden dressing table. *What in Solomon's name is going on?* Henry picked the letter up and examined it before opening.

To Henry,

My sincerest apologies for the abrupt manner that you were brought here, but as you can imagine it was necessary for the purposes of expediency. Wilmslow's people were waiting by the dock and would certainly have caught you; I had no way of knowing if you'd trust me as we had not spoken. You will be perfectly safe on the journey. As far as all aboard are concerned, you are just another paying customer. Enjoy the voyage and sorry for your loss.

Please see in the drawer below this table a modest contribution to help you on your way. And please send your mother my regards.

William Shakespeare

Henry stared at the letter, head swirling with questions. *Why*

would that cold, old man help me? How did he know my mother?
Why would he want to go against Wilmslow? How did he know
about Joan?

Henry opened the drawer, took out a pouch and opened it.
Three gold coins – not quite as much as the bird would have
been worth but far more money than Henry had ever had
before, and certainly enough for him to survive in Venice while
he looked for his mother. He smiled, even though terrible pain
came over him as he thought of Joan, and he wondered what
had happened to Mary and even to Matthew. He prayed and
sent a blessing and a farewell to Joan, and he prayed that Mary
was well too; he would miss her.

Hunger and the feeling of being cramped started to overcome
him, so Henry opened his cabin door and walked out onto the
deck. The ship was much more pleasant than Graham had
made out to be. There were indeed tough-looking sailors, and
the men rowing the ship looked as if they had not eaten in days
and were being forced to row as punishment, but there were
also a few wealthy people, girls selling produce like at the
theatre and men of the upper-middling sort playing cards. It
reminded Henry of London – if you had money it could be
great, if you did not, you were stuffed.

Henry looked back at the city fading in the distance: London.
He would miss it terribly, despite its stink and its vices. It was
the only place he had ever known. As the city disappeared,
Henry felt torn between the pain of losing Joan and the
excitement of his new adventure. The last two lines of his

sonnet suddenly came to him.

> *But risk it is worth to see all this earth*
> *People are people, thus we are not birds.*

The smell of salt water overtook the city's fading stench. Henry was going to get away from that stink, once and for all.

> *The bird and the ship, the ship and the bird*
> *One that is free because of its nature*
> *The bird and the ship, the ship and the bird*
> *One is man-made, thus destined to failure*
> *The birds can just fly, they don't even think*
> *Don't drop from the sky nor crash their fine tails*
> *Ships crash and capsize, they burn and they sink*
> *Just a few trees held together by nails*
> *The Bird and Ship, what's freedom and meaning*
> *Our ships move only with wind or labour*
> *The bird does not try, flying is breathing*
> *The cost of ship is death to the sailor*
> *But risk it is worth to see all this earth*
> *People are people, thus we are not birds.*

Henry felt a touch on his arm and he knew it was Mary even before he turned around to look.

*She smiles through a frown. The boy will find his way and
yet still she fears for him and prays to Olokun, God
of the oceans, to keep him safe. She waits, she prays,
she hopes the curse can be fought now that her manchild
has left the land of the strangers. She is ready to love the
child she has always loved and guided, though never known
in the flesh. She dreams of holding him close and smelling
his hair. A pang of terror strikes her.*

*What if he does not understand? What if he comes here only
to reject and scold her for not doing as a mother should?*

*She pushes these thoughts aside and thanks Oludumare, the
supreme creator, for keeping him from harm. She begs Shango
to give him strength for the next stage of his journey.
She vows to keep her magic eye watching over the boy.*

Elizabethan Street Slang

Apple-squire—Pimp

Autem—Church

Autem-mort—A married, female vagrant

Ay—Yes

Base—An insult of social position

Bate—Strife or Discord

Bedlam—Crazy

Bene—Good

Bousing ken—Alehouse

Breechless—An insult of social position

By my troth—A polite 'oath', suitable for women and children

By Solomon,

By St George—An emphatic oath

Caster—Cloak

Chaps—Mouth

Chief prigger—Head thief

Coney-catcher—Thief

Couch one's hogshead—To sleep

Cozen—To cheat or deceive

Crickets cry—Thought of as an omen of death

Cuttle-bung—Knife

Darkmans—Night

Dormouse valour—A little bravery

Doxy—Female vagabond, travelling usually with a man

Ear-kissing—Reaching the ear as rumours

Entreat—To encourage

Ethiope—A black person

Forsooth—Indeed

Fusty mucker—Old man

Gan—Mouth

Gleek—To jest or mock

Grace for grace—Favour in return for favour

High-sighted—Ambitious

Jackdaw—Loud, obnoxious person

Jigger—Door

Kissed off—Dead

Knave—An insult of social position

Lightmans—Day

Lour—Money

Lugs—Ears

Mill a ken—To rob a house

Mort—Old woman

Nay—No

Newgate nightingale—Prisoner

Nothing jealous—To have no doubt

Orb—Poetic word for world

Out of charge—Wrong

Pock-eaten—An insult meaning ugly

Prancer—Horse

Prigger—Thief

Quick mettle—Mentally sharp

Rascal, **Rascally**—An insult of social position

Rogue—An insult of social position

Rome-bouse—Wine

Rome-mort—The Queen

Romeville—London

Shells—Money

Simple—Medicinal herb

Sooth—Truth

Stamps—Legs

Stampers—Shoes

Skew—Cup

Stews—Brothel

Suitably trimmed—Well dressed

Tallow hatch—An insult to women

Tilly-vally—Nonsense

Turn Turk—To turn bad

Author's Note

This is a work of historical fiction. Any allusions to real historical people and events must be understood through that lens.

The book contains many, perhaps surprising, specific historical details. For example, shops in Elizabethan London really did have strange titles that gave no idea of what kinds of goods or services they provided. So a baker's might well be called The Red Lion. In the bear pit, they really did put monkeys on horseback and fed them to the dogs, and there really was a camel in a house on London Bridge.

The violence, the punishments, the rotten body parts above the city gates – all of that really did happen.

The style of speech is not fully Elizabethan as I felt that would not make for an entertaining read, but all of the street slang used is real Elizabethan street slang.

Some references to real events have been compressed for plot purposes. For example, the attempt to force the Moors from London happened in 1596. The Dutch Church libel – as it's become known – was in 1593 and the first showing of Hamlet was not until 1600. In our story they all happen during one summer.

Some geography is precise; in other places changing the

London map ever so slightly aided the story: for example, Paris Garden was actually past the Globe if you were walking over London Bridge. I would not want you to mistake creative licence for a lack of fact checking! Though I don't claim to be an Elizabethan historian.

If you are interested in reading further on the Elizabethan era, the books I found most useful were:

The Time Traveller's Guide to Elizabethan England by Ian Mortimer
Elizabeth's London by Liza Picard
The Black Tudors by Miranda Kaufmann
Playgoing in Shakespeare's London by Andrew Gurr
The Soul of the Age by Jonathan Bate
1599 by James Shapiro
The Elizabethan Underworld by A.V. Judges
The Elizabethan Underworld by Gāmini Salgādo
Shakespeare's Words by David Crystal

Acknowledgements

Thanks to Anne McNeil for all her support and the whole team at Hodder Children's. A special thank you to my editor, Ruth Girmatsion, who was a great collaborator all through this project. Thanks also to Catherine Coe, John C. Miles and Emma Roberts. And thanks to my manager Chanelle Newman. Thanks to Lavar Bullard for feedback and criticism on the very earliest (and most fragile) stages of this idea. And most importantly thanks to you, the reader.